"Let's just say I have a weakness for babies."

Ike turned to look at Marta with unabashed surprise. But it wasn't in her nature to stand idly by when someone needed help, and there had to be some decency in Ike, since he was so willing to take in his sister's child.

"And I also have a weakness for people who are willing to take on responsibilities," she added.

"Is that the way to your heart?"

"Leave my heart out of this." She didn't want him misunderstanding her motive for doing this. "Take it or leave it."

"I'll take it." Ike said. "I never look a gift horse in the mouth. That goes double for a beautiful angel of mercy."

Dear Reader,

Happy Anniversary! We're kicking off a yearlong celebration in honor of Silhouette Books' 20th Anniversary, with unforgettable love stories by your favorite authors, including Nora Roberts, Diana Palmer, Sherryl Woods, Joan Elliott Pickart and many more!

Sherryl Woods delivers the first baby of the new year in *The Cowboy and the New Year's Baby,* which launches AND BABY MAKES THREE: THE DELACOURTS OF TEXAS. And return to Whitehorn, Montana, as Laurie Paige tells the story of an undercover agent who comes home to protect his family and finds his heart in *A Family Homecoming,* part of MONTANA MAVERICKS: RETURN TO WHITEHORN.

Next is Christine Rimmer's tale of a lady doc's determination to resist the charming new hospital administrator. Happily, he proves irresistible in *A Doctor's Vow,* part of PRESCRIPTION: MARRIAGE. And don't miss Marie Ferrarella's sensational family story set in Alaska, *Stand-In Mom.*

Also this month, Leigh Greenwood tells the tale of two past lovers who must be *Married by High Noon* in order to save a child. Finally, opposites attract in *Awakened By His Kiss,* a tender love story by newcomer Judith Lyons.

Join the celebration; treat yourself to all six Special Edition romance novels each month!

Best,

Karen Taylor Richman
Senior Editor

Please address questions and book requests to:
Silhouette Reader Service
U.S.: 3010 Walden Ave., P.O. Box 1325, Buffalo, NY 14269
Canadian: P.O. Box 609, Fort Erie, Ont. L2A 5X3

MARIE FERRARELLA

STAND-IN MOM

SPECIAL EDITION

Published by Silhouette Books

America's Publisher of Contemporary Romance

To Alan Malunao, Jr.,
who would never have moved to Alaska,
even on a bet

SILHOUETTE BOOKS

ISBN 0-373-24294-8

STAND-IN MOM

Copyright © 1999 by Marie Rydzynski-Ferrarella

This edition published by arrangement with Harlequin Books S.A.

® and TM are trademarks of Harlequin Books S.A., used under license. Trademarks indicated with ® are registered in the United States Patent and Trademark Office, the Canadian Trade Marks Office and in other countries.

Visit us at www.romance.net

Printed in U.S.A.

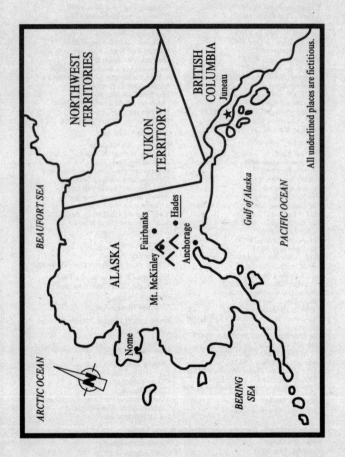

All underlined places are fictitious.

Chapter One

"Oh, my God, Sydney, just look at you!"

There was very little that could catch Marta Jensen off guard. Until this moment, she would have felt safe in saying that after teaching overenergized nine-year-olds for the last three years at Alderwood School, there was nothing that could surprise her enough to cause her mouth to drop open like a slow-witted cartoon character.

But seeing her best friend since college in her seventh month of pregnancy, looking as if she'd swallowed not one but possibly two beach balls, negated that. Marta stared, in wonder and in glee, all without consciously being aware that she was doing it.

The carry-on suitcase she'd toted down with her

slipped from Marta's fingers, landing with a *thud* on the floor and just barely missing contact with her toes, as she flung her arms around Sydney Elliot.

Sydney Kerrigan now, Marta mentally amended, blinking back tears of pure delight and joy, something else she hadn't thought she was capable of. But she'd missed this dear, wonderful friend, missed her with a passion she seldom allowed herself to feel. It had been much too long since she had seen her.

And was there a lot to see now, she thought, as Sydney's belly pressed against her in a hug.

"Sydney, wow," was all she could manage. It was one thing to intellectually know that Sydney was pregnant; it was another to see it for herself. Sydney had sent long, glowing letters about her life and her condition, but nothing took the place of actually seeing her best friend rounded out with child.

Marta sucked in her breath as Sydney's baby gave her a swift kick.

Laughing, sniffling, Marta stood back just enough to get another look at Sydney. Amazement hung on tenaciously. Sydney, pregnant. Sydney, a mother.

Well, she was already that, Marta reminded herself, thanks to the two children Shayne and his late wife had had. But still, it was going to take an awful lot of getting used to for her.

Marta kept her hands laced through both of Sydney's, as if afraid that if she lost that contact, Sydney would just disappear. She'd missed her a great deal this last year, so much more than even she would have thought. Outwardly gregarious, Marta had learned long ago not to make any attachments. Too many people had come and gone from her life.

But Sydney had been different. Sydney had been like the sister she'd always wanted. The family she'd never had. That was why she'd abruptly decided to make use of the break that the year-round school where she taught, with its eight-weeks-on, two-weeks-off schedule offered, conquer her fear of flying and come out to see Sydney. She hadn't quite managed to conquer the fear, but seeing Sydney had been worth enduring the unsettling, panicky feeling that had accompanied her all the way from Omaha.

It was still hard for her to assimilate. Marta had only recently gotten herself to believe and accept that over a year ago solid, steadfast Sydney had actually uprooted her life, sold off most of her possessions and come out to Alaska. To a town that could easily have fit into any corner of any one of Omaha's myriad of neighborhoods, and done it with room to spare. And now she was the wife and assistant of the only doctor for a hundred miles.

Maybe it shouldn't be so hard to assimilate, Marta mused. A year ago Sydney had made up her mind to start a new life somewhere else, and Sydney had always known what she wanted.

Sydney had always had purpose, direction. Unlike me, Marta thought ruefully.

Her eyes swept over her friend. Nearly seven months pregnant, Sydney carried her unborn child with the same grace that she carried herself. Tears persisted in gathering, smarting Marta's eyes.

This was silly. Tears were for sadness, and this was a happy time. Marta blinked them away and shook her head in wonder. "I'm sorry, I still can't believe you're pregnant."

Sydney laughed. "What, that kick didn't convince you?" Slipping one hand from Marta's, Sydney placed it over her swollen belly. "Whoever is in there is going to be born alert and running. I've got enough activity going on inside me for two babies."

Marta grasped Sydney's hand again, her eyes wide. "You're not carrying—"

"No." The denial was quick, firm and accompanied with just a slight shudder. "Shayne says there's only one unruly occupant in there." Grinning at the chilling, mixed blessing of a multiple birth, Sydney rolled her eyes. "Please, I've got my hands full with Sara and Mac. Two new babies would be more than I think I could sanely handle."

Sydney always underestimated herself, Marta thought. She was thoroughly convinced that Sydney could handle anything that life threw her way. Sydney had already proved that twice over, bouncing back from not one failed relationship, but two.

Too bad bouncing back wasn't contagious, Marta thought before firmly dismissing the subject. She was here to enjoy her visit with Sydney, however brief, to catch up on Sydney's life here, not dwell on her own past.

"That's why I'm here," Marta reminded her. "To help you 'handle' as much as I can in the next two weeks. And now that I've made my maiden flight, I'll be back the very next vacation." Marta smiled down at the swell of Sydney's belly. "To be here when you give birth to that bundle you're carting around—or shortly thereafter."

Sydney had never asked Marta outright to come to Alaska—only said how much she wished her friend could be here and see the place for herself. Marta had never before been off the ground, choosing to take any overland route available to where she wanted to go. Sydney knew what making this trip had cost Marta and was grateful beyond words that she had come. She couldn't imagine anyone she would have wanted in her corner more than Marta—with the exception of Shayne.

It had been a little over a year since she had last seen Marta. Then they had parted with Marta's reluctant good wishes ringing in her ears and Marta's dubious expression imprinted on her mind. Sydney knew that Marta had expected her to return to Omaha on the very next flight. When things abruptly turned sour on her, she almost had. But refusing to be defeated by the disappointment she'd initially discovered, Sydney had dug in and stayed.

Now, she was eternally grateful that she hadn't turned around and come back to what had then been home to her. Glad that she'd remained here to make a life for herself.

Several lives, she amended silently, affection filling her as she passed her hand over her belly and thought of the child she and Shayne had created. And of the children they would create in the future. It was a good life. A life that she knew Marta would love if only she gave it half a chance.

She meant to try to convince her of that every opportunity she found. More than anyone, Marta deserved to finally be happy.

But first things first. Marta had to get settled in, Sydney thought. *Then* she could begin working on her.

The taller of the two, Sydney slipped an arm around Marta's shoulders. "I can't tell you how glad I am that you finally decided to bite the bullet and come out here."

Marta curved her mouth—a generous mouth for a woman whose other features were so delicate—in amusement. "A little healthy panic never hurt anyone, I guess. Besides, I couldn't stand not being able to see you like this for myself, at least once."

Excited over seeing Marta again, Sydney had completely forgotten about the man who had accompanied her in the Cessna on the trip over here—until he cleared his throat. Loudly and with amusement.

Sydney flushed warmly as she turned toward him. His easygoing smile only made her feel worse for the oversight. "Where are my manners? Marta, this is—"

Marta held her hand up, stopping Sydney's introduction in mid-sentence. Though leery of good-looking men the way only a woman who has been badly burned could be, she still had never been slow in appreciating the sight of one. And this one was good-looking with a capital *G-L*. Tall, and obviously muscular beneath the unzipped parka he had on, he had an olive complexion and cheekbones that could set the rhythm of a woman's heart off by several beats. There was no question in Marta's mind that the man with jet-black hair standing behind Sydney was nothing short of drop-dead gorgeous.

Just as Sydney had told her he would be.

"Yes, I know who he is." Marta moved forward, throwing her arms around the man who looked a little surprised, as well as faintly amused, at her declaration. She liked the way he smiled. Damn, but Sydney was lucky. "Sydney said you'd be the most devastatingly handsome man at the airport."

Momentarily overcome with emotion, Marta hugged just a tad harder. Sydney looked happy, and her letters had fairly sung of contentment. Any man who could do that for her best friend earned Marta's unqualified affection and gratitude. "I thought she was exaggerating, but it looks like for once in her life, Sydney was making an understatement."

On her toes, Marta gave Sydney's companion what she felt was an appropriate, friendly kiss in greeting, her enthusiasm and happiness getting the better of her.

That Ike LeBlanc was surprised to have a petite, attractive redhead all but wrap herself around him within five minutes of their first meeting was putting it mildly. That this same woman then went on to kiss him with enthusiasm only compounded that surprise.

But Ike was never one to be caught off guard for more than a single heartbeat. Responding to stimuli faster than any clinical biochemist could ever have prayed for, Ike wrapped his arms around the woman's trim, tempting frame and hugged her with the same enthusiasm she had displayed.

He returned not only the hug, but the kiss as well. With verve. If she was going to catch him in a lip lock, then he damn well was going to make it worth both their whiles.

With a barely perceptible sound of pleasure escaping, Ike tightened his embrace and deepened the kiss that God and this woman had chosen to bestow on him. Deepened it and felt his blood warming to an incredible, tantalizing degree. With the shortage of women in not only Hades, but in Alaska itself, he didn't get to do this nearly as often as he would have liked. He was *not* about to throw the opportunity away.

For the briefest of seconds, Marta's head swirled and her pulse throbbed, as her very skin heated to the temperature of a much sought-after hot springs in this February wilderness. Her body melted in response, and had begun molding against his when her brain finally caught up to the rest of her, issuing orders like a strict commandant. She reeled in sheer horror, disgust and embarrassment.

What was going on here? This was Sydney's husband for heaven's sake, and he was kissing her as if they had been intimate with one another all their lives.

What was even worse was that she had just kissed him back.

Appalled, Marta wedged her hands up against the man's chest, shoving him away as hard as she could to break contact.

Coming up for air, Marta felt her jaw slacken as, for the second time in a matter of minutes, her mouth dropped open in overwhelmed surprise. The power of speech was temporarily and completely beyond her grasp. She could only stare at the man who had just effectively destroyed her cherished belief that no matter what, time moved relentlessly forward. It hadn't moved on. For one tiny moment there, it had stood perfectly still, content to linger and hear nothing but the pounding of her heart and the soft sound made by her knees as they dissolved.

Chagrined and heartbroken for Sydney, as well as furious with this man who didn't deserve to be her husband, Marta searched vainly for her tongue. She would have slapped him with all her might if Sydney hadn't been standing right there, watching.

And how could she be standing there, watching,

when her husband had all but seduced her best friend in a crowded airport?

Questions, oaths and outrage all scrambled through her mind. Marta swung around to face Sydney, apologies mingling with denouncements pulsating in her brain.

To her overwhelming surprise, Sydney looked completely unfazed. Maybe even a little amused and pleased. What was the matter with her? Had the overwhelmingly cold weather frozen her brain and snapped her brittle self-respect? Sydney's husband was in the same shameful category as Alex Kelley had been.

"Sydney, don't you mind?" Marta cried in dazed wonder.

The question struck Sydney as odd. "Why should I mind? Unless, of course, you didn't like it."

Although, Sydney thought, that hardly seemed likely. In the time she'd been here, Sydney had never met a single woman who complained about being kissed by Ike LeBlanc. Complained about not being kissed by Ike was more like it. Ike, with his dark good looks and his warm, sexy smile was what every woman's dreams were made of. With the affection of an indulgent sister, Sydney was very surprised it hadn't gone to his head. But sexy or not, Ike was well grounded, which was what made him so likable. And what made him Ike.

"Unless I didn't like it?" Marta repeated dumbly.

"Did you?" Ike asked as he looked at Marta, mildly amused by the strangely disoriented expression on her face. She wasn't alone in feeling that way. He had to admit that Sydney's friend had managed to scramble more than one circuit on his motherboard with her kiss. Sweet and almost seductively submissive, the kiss had knocked him for a loop.

That rarely happened.

The lady bore scrutiny. A great deal of close scrutiny, he promised himself.

"No, I didn't," Marta said, squaring her shoulders. It was a bald-faced lie, but it was the only admission he was going to get out of her, the monster. What was he looking for, accolades? With his wife, ripe with his baby, standing almost at his elbow? Her eyes narrowed, shooting daggers at him. "And that's not the point!"

Confused, Sydney and Ike exchanged looks. Sydney raised a single shoulder, then let it fall, silently letting him know that she had no more clue as to what was going on than he did.

She looked at Marta, completely bewildered. She knew all about Marta's one failed, traumatic venture into love. Knew, too, that Marta's heart, so eager to love, had been repeatedly bruised during her childhood when she had been passed around from one foster home to another. She'd had more than enough to overcome.

Had something else happened in the last year that

Marta hadn't written to her about? "What is the point, Marta?" Sydney asked.

"The point—" Marta felt as if she were strangling on her anger. She huffed, then began again. "The point is that your husband kissed me as if…as if…" She couldn't find the words to define what had just happened here. "Well, he just kissed me." Anyone with eyes could have seen just how.

Sydney looked around, half expecting to see Shayne appear. But that wasn't possible. Still, Marta looked deadly serious.

"Shayne? When?"

Marta threw up her hands, exasperated. Was Sydney blind?

"Now." She waved a disparaging hand at Ike. "Here." For heaven's sake, Sydney had been looking straight at her, at *them,* when it happened.

It was only then that Sydney grinned again, understanding flooding through her. Grinned while Ike laughed. The only one not in on the joke was Marta. But by the way Sydney was looking at Ike, she was definitely getting an inkling.

In a voice that was deadly still and steely, she asked, "You're not Shayne?" knowing the answer before he said a word.

Searching for breath, unable to form a word yet, Ike could only shake his head in reply. No wonder she'd looked so upset. She thought her best friend's husband was hitting on her. The very thought of Shayne ever doing anything remotely improper was utterly amusing to Ike. Shayne was as good as they came. The man would die as soon as look at another woman in anything but a professional capacity. His heaven began and ended with Sydney, and Ike envied his friend more than a little. It was something he'd never experienced himself.

"I'm sorry, Marta." Sydney struggled to catch her breath. The last thing she wanted was for Marta to think she was laughing at her. "This is my fault. I never sent you photographs of Shayne. The ones from the wedding were lost," she explained with a trace of sorrow, "and I never got around to getting a new camera after the moose stepped on mine. Long story," she added quickly in response to the questioning look on Marta's face. She placed a hand on Marta's shoulder, silently entreating her not to be angry. "I'm really sorry. I guess when you saw him with me—"

Tactfully, Sydney avoided referring to Marta's comment about Ike's looks. And when you came right down to it, she thought, Ike and Shayne did look a great deal alike. Both men were tall, both had dark hair—although Ike's was darker—and both were as handsome as any woman could pray for. She could see why Marta had made the mistake.

"I just assumed he was Shayne," Marta concluded for Sydney.

That still didn't excuse the man for kissing a stranger as if she were his long-lost love, Marta thought ruefully. Her body temperature still hadn't returned to normal. But now it was annoyance, rather than any physical response, that was the cause.

Turning, Marta stood waiting for enlightenment. "Who are you, anyway?"

"A very blessed errand boy, darlin'." With a flourish, Ike bowed grandly. The engaging grin he flashed shot straight into her like a bulb exploding in a dark room when the light switch was first thrown.

"Shayne couldn't make it," Sydney explained quickly. "He had a medical emergency at the last minute, and he absolutely didn't want me flying alone."

There'd been no choice, really. Shayne was at the Inuit village, taking care of their housekeeper's youngest grandson, who had suddenly come down with pneumonia. That was the only reason he'd reluctantly allowed her to fly to Anchorage instead of piloting the plane himself. Sydney was the only other pilot in the area—thanks to his lessons—and there was no way she could come to meet Marta's plane if she didn't fly in herself. There was also no way she would have allowed Marta to land without someone being there to meet her. As it was, she and Ike had been late in arriving because of unexpected turbulence.

"Marta, this is Klondyke LeBlanc, Shayne's best friend and owner of the Salty Saloon," Sydney added. "He was kind enough to fill in for Shayne and come with me to the airport."

"Part owner," Ike amended. The other half belonged to his cousin, Jean Luc, who had been dragged into the business venture almost against his will. But Ike had thought it a sound investment, the first of several eventually, and he had wanted Luc to share in the profits. And the future.

As if they hadn't just kissed with more passion than propriety only moments earlier, Ike politely held out his hand to Marta. "My friends all call me Ike."

Her lips forming a reproving frown, Marta placed her hand in his with all the feeling of a woman coming in contact with a reptile. A poisonous one at that. The last thing she wanted right now was a new friend whose kisses tasted like sin served up on a silver platter. There was already far too much on that platter for her to deal with at the moment without adding another complication.

Marta inclined her head, distant but polite. "Hello, Mr. LeBlanc."

He read her message loud and clear. But living in Hades all his life, Ike had never been one to be intimidated by frost.

"Oh, don't be that way, darlin'. After all, you were the one who kissed me—at least at first," he added gallantly. His brown eyes were fairly shining with unsuppressed amusement. "I just enjoyed the ride. Can't fault a man for that."

Her eyes briefly locked with his.

"Yes," Marta replied mildly, showing no emotion whatsoever, "I can."

Sydney wasn't fooled. She knew that beneath

Marta's polite exterior, her best friend was seething. This was not an auspicious beginning, but there definitely was hope. Sydney had her work cut out for her. She threaded her arm through Marta's and looked over her shoulder at Ike.

"Why don't you see about getting Marta's luggage for her, Ike?" She nodded toward the luggage carousel, by now completely depleted except for two suitcases she recognized as Marta's. "Don't worry," she assured Ike with a smile that was nothing short of conspiratorial. "Marta could never hold a grudge."

Marta merely smiled. Oh, yes, she could, Marta thought, if she was humiliated. She hadn't come out here to deal with some strange man, especially a good-looking, unattached Don Juan.

"You've been away for a year," Marta reminded Sydney, her smile enigmatic.

Time made no difference. Sydney knew Marta's heart.

"Some things," Sydney allowed with confidence, "never change."

And other things, Marta thought, unconsciously glancing back at Ike and his wide grin, did.

Chapter Two

"You look a little pale, darlin'," Ike said, frowning. Flying was second nature to him, but obviously not to the woman all but nestled beside him in the tight space that comprised the Cessna's back seat, her face whiter than the pristine snow that lay several thousand feet below them—and growing steadily whiter. Her breathing was beginning to sound shallow.

He wondered if she was claustrophobic. Ike remembered seeing the same pallid color on his uncle, who had been claustrophobic. After being trapped in a cave-in at the mine, the man had never been quite right in his head until the day he died.

Following his instincts, Ike reached for Marta's hand and took it in his. Jerking, she turned away

from the window she'd just glanced out of and
looked at him. Her eyes were wide and a little wild,
but mostly they were accusing. He covered the hand
he held with his other one.

Marta pulled her hand away from him. Fighting
for composure, she took a shaky breath. It didn't
help. The plane's rattling noise sounded like a death
knell. Knees locked, Marta moved forward on her
seat, her eyes fastened to Sydney's profile. How
could she look so calm? Couldn't she hear the
noise? Or could that horrible sound possibly be normal?

She fervently prayed that it was.

"No offense, Sydney, but are you sure that this
thing is going to be able to hold together long
enough to get us back to your place?"

She'd been horrified when she first saw the plane
and was reminded that there was no other way to
reach Hades this time of year. But she had tried her
best to appear unfazed by the ordeal she faced.

Being engulfed by the ordeal was another matter.

Momentarily turning from the view of the perfect
sky before her, Sydney flashed Marta an encour-
aging smile. Poor Marta. She could remember her
own first reaction to Shayne's plane. She'd been
sure they were going to die before she ever got to
Hades. But the plane, for all its unique noises, was
as sound as the little foreign car Marta loved so
well.

Sounder, Sydney was willing to bet. Shayne had
just gone over it with a fine-tooth comb last week-

end in one of those rare islands of time that usually eluded them. He'd pronounced the craft safe enough for her to use.

Which was good, because Sydney loved flying. To her it was like becoming one with the air—the closest thing to gliding through the clouds on her own power, unencumbered. It was a rather nice feeling these days, considering the weight she was carrying around when she walked.

"Don't let the noise fool you," she told Marta gently. For emphasis, Sydney patted the dashboard. "This is a very sturdy plane."

"It sounds as if it's about to rattle apart at any second."

"All small planes have their own melody." Sydney shifted back around in her seat. "Distract her, Ike."

Now there was an instruction Ike would have loved to follow. But he seldom went where he wasn't welcome, and Sydney's friend did not look welcoming. Yet. "Much as I'd dearly love to comply, darlin', I don't think your friend wants to be distracted by me at the moment."

If it hadn't been for Alex messing up Marta's life so badly, Sydney thought, mentally calling down curses on the other man's unworthy head, Marta would have been more than receptive to Ike and his easygoing charm. It would do Marta a world of good to be around someone like Ike. Whether by a word, a look or something far more intimate, Ike had the gift of making women of all ages feel special.

But Alex Kelley had done a number on her friend, taking her heart and using it as a basketball to be played with anytime he was on home court. His faithfulness lasted as long as his attention span, which, as Sydney recalled, had never been very great. The breakup had happened shortly after she'd left Omaha. Sydney wished she could have been there for Marta. Despite everything, she knew how hard it must have been for her to end the two-year relationship, especially after investing so much of her heart in it.

Because of him, Marta had sworn off any and all men, which was a crying shame. Marta had a huge heart and a great deal of love to give. To the right man.

"Don't worry about me, Sydney. I'm all right."

Marta would sound far more convincing if her voice wasn't shaking, Sydney thought. "We'll be there before you know it," she promised.

Too late for that, Marta thought nervously. She was trying very hard not to look down, but she couldn't seem to help herself. The snow looked so soft, but it wouldn't be if they fell out of the sky.

With the window on one side and Ike on the other, there was nowhere for her to look but straight ahead. At oblivion. That didn't help, either.

Marta moistened her lips with the last bit of saliva she had. Her throat felt as if it were closing up.

"Are you positive there isn't any other way to get to Hades?"

"Positive." It was Ike, the native, not Sydney, who answered. "At least, not in the winter." It was one of the things that had driven so many people, including his own sister, Juneau, out of Hades. The isolation. "The snow blocks the roads for weeks at a time. We become our own little world out here."

Marta shivered and looked at Sydney. "That kind of makes Shayne and you like Tarzan and Jane, except with snow." Her cosmopolitan heart would get cabin fever within a week. "How can you stand that?"

Again it was Ike who answered her. "Oh, it has its advantages." For instance, he knew he surely wouldn't have minded being snowed in somewhere with the petite woman sharing the back seat with him.

What did it take to melt her down? he wondered. To turn that iciness she was displaying toward him into fire? If he knew his women—and he liked to think without any undue vanity that he did—there was a warm, quite possibly even passionate, woman somewhere beneath that No Trespassing sign she wore so boldly.

It was, he mused, definitely a challenge. One he wouldn't mind taking on.

Ever since he could remember, Ike had always loved women. All women. In his opinion there was something of beauty to be found within every woman, no matter who. It just took the right man to find a way to bring that beauty out. He had no idea why he'd been blessed the way he had, but he found himself endowed with that ability—to make the most somber of women smile, to find their charms, hidden or otherwise, and make them aware of it. Grateful for it. Women always seemed to bloom around him, and he never bothered denying that he had a grand weakness for flowers.

But this flower was going to need a little cultivating, he thought as he silently studied her. She was going to require a little careful feeding to make her open up. She made him think of a blossom that had not been properly nurtured. Certainly not properly appreciated.

Ike made a mental note to ask Sydney a few pertinent questions about her friend at the first opportunity.

"Advantages?" Marta echoed in disbelief. What kind of advantages could there possibly be to being snowed in and cut off from everything? She ran her hands up along her arms, as if that would ward off the chill that went far deeper than any outside cold could create. "I don't see how." Knowing it had to sound critical, she still couldn't help the question that rose to her lips. "How do you keep from going stir-crazy?"

Ike smiled broadly. His eyes took slow, languid measure of her, moving down her body like a warm breath. "Oh, there are ways to occupy yourself in Hades."

It seemed impossible, given the temperature, but

she felt herself growing warm. It was almost as if he were looking right through her heavy parka and the bulky sweater and jeans she wore beneath. Looking right at the red silk undergarments she had on.

"Yeah, I'll bet." Trying her best to shut this man and his X-ray eyes out, Marta leaned forward in her seat again. "Are you sure you should be flying in your condition, Sydney?"

The question made Sydney smile broadly. Those had been Shayne's exact words to her this morning. It had been the husband, not the doctor, who had asked them. She was right at the cut-off point, even though she'd declared that she was more than capable of making the run. Though she was accustomed to being independent, the concern that motivated Shayne had warmed her, reminding her just how much she loved the man fate had thrown into her life.

She glanced down at the steering wheel that was all but resting on her protruding belly.

"Right now, I'd say I can fly a lot better than I can walk," Sydney said, sighing. "No one told me how badly I'd be listing when I reached my last couple of months."

"You don't list, darlin', you just glide a little less swiftly, that's all," Ike assured Sydney with a soft laugh that seemed, at least to Marta, to seductively fill the small cabin. "But a hundred babies wouldn't rob you of your grace, and you know it."

Though she was trying vainly to ignore him,

Marta couldn't help looking at Ike, a bemused expression on her face. Her eyes shifted toward the back of Sydney's head. "Does he talk like this all the time?"

"Most of it." Sydney laughed. The man had a very special place in her heart. He had been the one not only to encourage her to stay, but to point out that Shayne was struggling very hard not to fall in love with her. If it hadn't been for Ike, she might have moved back to Omaha and missed out on the very best portion of her life. "Isn't he lovely?" She spared a glance in his direction. "Don't know what I'd do without Ike sometimes."

"Don't tease me like that, darlin'," he warned playfully, "or you'll tempt me to do away with the best friend I ever had." Hands on the back of the seat in front of him, Ike smiled warmly at Sydney. "If he ever stops paying you the attention you so richly deserve, you know where to come."

Sydney's laugh was short, amused. As if the man would ever betray a friend. She knew him far too well to ever believe that. If she ever did have a falling out with Shayne, Ike would be the first one there trying to talk them back together—and not giving up until they reconciled. "Big talk coming from a confirmed bachelor."

"Oh, no, not confirmed." He looked at Marta and winked. "Just waiting for the right woman to come along, that's all."

There was a great deal more to the story than that, Sydney thought. And even if there hadn't been, she seriously doubted that Ike would give up the place of honor he held in all women's hearts for a place of honor in the heart of just one.

Still, there might be a chance, she mused, catching a whiff of the light scent that Marta liked to put on before she donned a stitch of clothing.

The plane groaned like a keening woman in deep mourning. Marta felt that if she were any more rigid, she would snap like a frozen twig. "Is it much farther?"

"We'll be there soon," Sydney promised.

It couldn't be soon enough for Marta.

Marta wasn't aware of grasping his hand. To her, Ike's hand was part of the armrest—until she felt his fingers close over hers. But her breath had completely escaped her lungs at that point, and there were no words with which to upbraid him or even to say a single scathing thing about his obstinately being too familiar with her.

Marta was sure this was going to be her last moment on earth, and she didn't want to enter the next world with a curse on her lips.

God didn't like it when you cursed.

For a little thing, she sure had a hell of a grip, Ike thought, feeling his fingers go numb. It was a bumpy landing as far as landings went, with a spate of unexpected tailwind turning on them at the very last minute. As the plane was being buffeted by the wind, coming in for the final leg of its journey, Ike was certain that Marta was going to pass out right where she sat.

But then, taking another look into her bright green eyes, he'd amended that. The woman looked like the type to spit in the devil's eye rather than let him know she was afraid. He liked that. It showed character, and he was a great admirer of character.

When it looked as if she was going to snap off the armrest, he'd slipped his hand into hers again, knowing that she'd probably take his head off for it when she could talk again. But his desire to offer her a measure of comfort transcended any apprehension over words she might use to cut him down. He never liked to see someone in pain, physical or mental.

"It's okay," he said softly. "Sydney's never crashed a plane yet."

"All it takes is once." Marta didn't know if she thought the words or said them out loud until she heard him laughing softly to himself.

Damn him anyway. She was descending into hell, and Don Juan was already with her.

"You can open your eyes now, we've landed," he whispered to her.

She was aware of his warm breath along her face before she attempted to make any sense out of the words that were buzzing close to her ear. Her eyes flew open. Embarrassed, she stiffened, then quickly pulled her hand away from his.

He had to think she was an idiot. That made two of them.

Avoiding Ike's eyes, Marta cleared her throat. "Sorry."

His shrug was careless, easy. "Nothing to be sorry for. Not everyone likes to fly."

He knew damn well what she was referring to. He was undoubtedly enjoying stringing this out. "I meant about squeezing your hand."

Ike pretended to examine his hand for signs of wear. His grin was fast and lethal and took no prisoners. "Hardly felt it. Feel free to squeeze anything you like anytime you have the need."

Color, quick and bright, flashed across her cheeks and face, working its way simultaneously to the roots of her dark red hair and down her throat. Marta could feel it, and by the look in his eyes knew that he could see it. She damned this one legacy from a mother she barely knew: translucent skin. It allowed her every emotion to be telegraphed so clearly. If she had skin his color—bronzed, she thought as if he had an intimate relationship with the elusive sun—no one would ever guess at what she was feeling.

Her eyes narrowed as she looked at him. "I won't be doing any squeezing." And that, she figured, got her message across loud and clear. She was here to visit Sydney and her family. There was no room in her schedule for penciled-in recreational activities that involved egotistical men.

He glossed over her words. "Then I'll be the poorer for it, darlin'."

Seeing Sydney reaching for the door, Ike opened his own and jumped down into the snow. Rounding the nose of the plane quickly, he presented himself at her side by the time she'd opened the door, ready to assist her from the plane.

Amusement played across Sydney's lips. "Looking to do a good deed?" she asked, as he carefully helped her from the plane. "Why don't you help—" She didn't have time to finish.

Disembarking from the plane, Marta found that her legs had suddenly transformed themselves from solid flesh and bone to rubbery oatmeal. She gasped as she found herself keeling over. Ike swung around and caught her before she fell face-first into the snow.

The feel of his arms, strong and sure, closing instantly around her, ignited Marta's indignation. It also created a spark of something else within her that ultimately went to fuel her indignation even more. She didn't like that hot, fast, upward spike she felt, didn't like it at all.

With a toss of her head, she sent the hood of her parka slipping off to rest on her shoulders. Hair the color of flame at twilight began a hopeless duel with the wind that was picking up. It was the wind, not proximity, that snatched her breath away, she told herself. Like a reigning gypsy queen, she raised her head regally. "I'm perfectly capable of standing up on my own."

Ike withdrew his hands, holding them aloft in the air like a man staring down the bore of a red-hot .44. "Anything you say, darlin'."

But she wasn't capable of standing up on her own. At least, not at the moment. Taking another step proved that. Feeling wobbly as well as chagrined, she threw her hand out and braced herself against the side of the Cessna. She regretted it instantly. The metal felt incredibly cold against her fingertips. She shoved her hand in her pocket, praying for the return of equilibrium.

In answer to her prayer, Ike took hold of her elbow as if he were escorting her onto the dance floor of her senior prom. "This happens sometimes with first-time flyers," he assured her easily. From her pallor and her questions, he took it for granted that this was her first time in a plane this size. "It takes a second or two to get your land legs back."

Grateful for the momentary respite, Marta tried to understand the strange feeling in her lower body. "I thought that was only with ships."

He grinned again. She wished he'd stop that.

Ike patted the side of the plane. "This *is* a ship." He glanced at Sydney, knowing that she agreed. "A ship of the air, and someday, when I have the time, this fine woman is going to teach me how to navigate it, aren't you?"

Pulling her parka as close around her as she could, Sydney began to lead the way to her house. It was only three, but it was growing dark already. Though she loved it here, she'd be glad when summer was more than just a distant memory. "You'd be better off having Shayne teach you."

Still holding firmly onto Marta's elbow, he hooked his other arm through Sydney's. He didn't want to risk having her fall. "You're underestimating yourself, darlin'. Besides—" his eyes danced "—you're a lot lovelier to look at than Shayne ever was."

Sydney knew it was just Ike's way of talking. Flattery, plain and simple. But there were times when she loved the sound of it. With a shake of her head, she sighed. "How is it that Shayne never learned to talk like you?"

His laugh was deep and hearty. Momentarily letting go of Marta's elbow, he raised his gloved finger to his lips.

"Sh, we don't make fun of the slow-witted." He took hold of Marta's elbow again without even looking her way. "Besides, he's the one you married, not me."

"You never asked," Sydney deadpanned.

It was his turn to sigh.

"I guess that makes me the slow-witted one then, doesn't it?" And then he turned his dark eyes toward Marta, the movement so unexpected that it caught her completely off guard. As did the gleam she saw in those eyes. Marta felt as if she'd suddenly been put on notice. "Maybe the fates have decided to give me a second chance by bringing your friend to my doorstep."

It took Marta a minute to rally, but rally she did.

She'd been in this place before, on the receiving end of a charmer's compliments. Roses with hidden thorns. She wasn't about to get scratched again.

"I believe we're approaching Sydney's doorstep, not yours," Marta said pointedly.

But rather than be put off the way she'd expected him to be, Ike merely nodded his approval as he glanced toward Sydney. "Beautiful and quick, too. They really do raise wonderful women in the lower forty-nine, don't they?"

Marta narrowed her eyes again. "Why don't you go there yourself and see?"

The wind whipped her hair against his cheek, evoking a warm feeling within him. "Maybe I will," he agreed. "Someday."

Sydney could only smile and shake her head at the exchange. If Ike had ever had any intention of leaving Hades, or Alaska itself for that matter—the way so many others did as soon as they reached legal age—he wouldn't have worked so hard to make a life for himself here.

He'd started out in his teens. Behind that devastating smile, Sydney had discovered, was a man with a plan. Ike had worked hard until he could purchase an interest in the local saloon. For some, that would have been enough. For Ike, it had only been a start.

One foothold had led to another until he was the owner, holding the title to the establishment along with the cousin he'd insisted on bringing in with him. Over the years, his holdings had increased.

Now he held the deed to more than one piece of real estate, with grand plans of expanding the town. He meant to bring civilization, and the next century, to Hades.

While melting the heart of every woman in Alaska.

"Ike would never leave us," Sydney told Marta matter-of-factly as they approached her front door. "All the women in the area would rise up in protest. They'd probably take over the airport just to keep him here." She was only half joking. The men far outnumbered the women here, but there was still a soft spot in each female heart for Ike LeBlanc.

"Ah, now, darlin', you're making me blush."

Making him blush, her foot. Marta frowned. She was well-acquainted with his type. All talk and a few magic tricks, smoke and mirrors, but no substance whatsoever. She'd been there, done that, and had had her heart irrevocably broken. The pieces of it had never been glued together properly.

But that was all right. She had no further use for that organ anyway. She certainly had no intention of ever falling in love again, so her heart's condition was no longer of any consequence.

Standing before the door, Sydney paused and turned toward Marta. "Okay, I want you to brace yourself."

"Why?" She wanted to get inside, out of the wind that was beginning to turn raw. And away from the man at her elbow. "Are you planning on taking me on another plane ride?"

"No." It was suddenly so important to Sydney that Marta like her children. Marta was like family. With Sydney's father gone, Marta was all the close family she had left, aside from Shayne and the children. "I just want you to be prepared for Sara and Mac."

Puzzled, Marta looked up at her. "I'm a teacher, same as you, Sydney. Meeting kids isn't exactly something out of the ordinary for me."

"No," Sydney agreed softly, "but these are mine."

Marta smiled. She understood. "Point well taken," she said as Sydney pushed open the oak door. Sara and Mac materialized with greetings, with hugs and with questions, surrounding Sydney as only two vital, energetic children under the age of twelve could.

Marta had a nice smile, Ike thought as he followed her in the opened door. He was going to have to see what he could do about bringing it out more often.

Chapter Three

Marta hadn't expected to feel an ache. Happiness, yes, to be sure. Happiness for her friend and for the life that Sydney had carved out for herself. Perhaps she'd even thought to feel a vicarious sense of sharing since she and Sydney had once shared everything, good times and bad.

But not an ache. Definitely not an ache.

Yet it was there, bittersweet and strangely acute, burrowing into her and hollowing her out before she managed to bank it down and lock it away. There, because what she was witnessing right before her encompassed everything she had always longed for herself, almost from the very first moment she drew breath. A home, a family. And children. They were all here, and all Sydney's.

A touch of envy raised its head before it, too, was sent away. This was Sydney's life, and Marta was ecstatic for her.

She just wished...

But there was no point to that. Her judgment as far as who to entrust her heart to was flawed. Best not to go there.

"What d'you bring me?" Sara's question had Marta focusing on the child.

Mac was on Sydney's other side, tugging at her arm. Tugging for her attention. "Did you get my CD?"

Sara lifted her head importantly. "She didn't have time to get your ol' CD, she was busy picking up the lady."

Their voices and questions mingled, encircling the mother they had adopted as fiercely as she had adopted them. Amid the noise was their unabashed, wide-eyed scrutiny of the new person dropped into their midst.

Marta felt as if she'd been taken apart and put back together again in an instant. And approved, judging from the expressions on the two upturned faces. Visitors, Sydney had warned her, were rare in Hades, especially this time of year. Any new face was to be evaluated and gone over like a shiny, brand-new possession, to be passed from hand to hand and admired, or criticized.

Abandoning their siege on Sydney, they turned their eyes toward Marta, competing for her attention.

"Are you gonna stay here forever?" Sara wanted to know. "Mommy said she couldn't wait until you got here."

Elbowing his sister out of the way, Mac presented himself front and center. At ten, he was already exhibiting the promise of becoming a handsome man, Marta thought.

"Did you know she was our mom now? Did she tell you about us?"

Giving her brother an impatient look, Sara tugged on Marta's parka sleeve. "Do you have any kids of your own we can play with?"

Mac grabbed her arm. "Can I show you my room?"

Not to be outdone, Sara caught hold of Marta's other arm and pulled in the opposite direction.

Stunned, tickled, Marta began to laugh. She was used to children, but as Sydney had promised, this was something special.

"Hold it, hold it." Knowing that if she laughed, she'd only undercut what she was about to say, Sydney bit back the sound. Instead, she raised her hand like a safety-patrol crossing guard. "Mac, Sara, let Marta catch her breath."

Much to Sara and Mac's delight, Marta shook her head, siding with them.

"Oh, no, don't let me catch my breath. This is great." Half in love with the overwhelming duo already, Marta flashed a smile at Sydney over their heads. "There're only two instead of thirty. I can manage, really." Looking down at the pair, she fired back answers to their questions. "No, I'm not going to stay here forever, but I will be here for a couple of weeks." From the corner of her eye, she saw Sydney's look of pleasure. "And I couldn't wait to get here myself." She thought of the Cessna's bumpy ride. "Although I wasn't so sure about the last leg of the trip."

Wispy bangs caught in tiny furrows as Sara scrooched her brow. "Do trips have legs?"

"That's just an expression she's using, darlin'," Ike interjected.

Marta noticed that the little girl preened at the endearment. Why shouldn't she? At seven, Sara didn't know any better. She hadn't at twenty-four, Marta thought ruefully. But she did now.

"And yes," Marta continued, running a hand over each silky head, "I know that she's your mom. Every single letter she's written to me since she got here has been full of things about you." The information pleased both children, who puffed up their chests importantly. "I don't have any kids of my own for you to play with, but I'll play with you myself if you let me." The declaration was received with unsuppressed excitement. "And I would love to see your rooms."

Quicker than her brother, Sara caught Marta's hand in hers first. "This way."

Sara might have been quicker, but Mac was stronger and more determined as he took the visitor's other hand and pulled her in the opposite direction. "No, she said she wanted to see my room."

Sydney hung her parka on the rack, throwing her blue scarf on top of it. She looked at Marta, her point proven.

"See what I mean by overwhelming?" She got in between the boy and girl. "Kids, let go of Marta, she's not a pull-toy or a wishbone." Reluctantly, they each let go of the hand they were holding. "She's going to be here for a while, so everyone'll get their turn with her."

"Does that include me?" Ike was behind her, gently helping her off with her parka before Marta could think to stop him.

Soft and low, his voice moved like a seductive, rich scent along the spring breeze. Surrounding her. The smile on his lips hit her with the force of a lightning bolt when she turned around to face him. Unprepared, she felt the definite crackle of electricity passing over her. Into her.

Gotta watch that, Marta, she warned herself. *You know what charmers are like.* The man obviously had had a lifetime to hone his skills of seduction, and, like the children, welcomed a new diversion.

Not this time, mister. This time, you've met your match. I've had my shots.

Like a referee stepping between two contenders to avoid unnecessary bloodshed, Sydney was quick to get between Marta and Ike. She took Marta's parka and hung it next to hers. "Ike volunteered to show you around when you feel like sightseeing."

I just bet he did, Marta thought. Because the children were there, she kept the comment that immediately occurred to her to herself. Instead, she smiled broadly at Sara and Mac, placing a hand on each of their shoulders.

"All the sights I came to see are right here in this room." She cast an offhanded glance in Ike's direction. "Besides, I'm here as a friend, not a tourist."

Sara's pretty face puckered again. "But how are you going to fall in love with Alaska if you don't see it?"

So, there was a plot afoot. And Sydney looked so innocent, pregnant and all. Marta raised a bemused brow in Sydney's direction. "I have no intention of falling in love with Alaska." Her eyes strayed toward Ike. "Or anything else."

Ike stepped in, the expression on his face one that any poker player would have envied. "Wasn't that the plan? To show her around and get her to stay?"

It had been what she'd hoped for, but nothing that Sydney had put into so many words. At least, not to anyone but Shayne. Obviously she was going to have to have a word with her husband about what the word *secret* meant.

"Ike."

He heard the warning note in Sydney's voice and grinned. "Let the cat out of the bag, didn't I?" His glance, all encompassing and appreciative, swept over Marta again before returning to Sydney. "Never mind, if it's meant to happen, it'll happen."

Marta had the very distinct impression that the tall saloon keeper wasn't talking about a love affair that had to do with frozen rivers and snow-covered mountains. Pointedly, she smiled up into his face. "Just as long as no one is holding their breath."

It wasn't his breath he was counting on holding, but a beautiful and quite possibly underappreciated woman, he mused. But for now, it was time to ease out of the range of fire.

"Well, you two ladies have a lot to catch up on, so I'll leave you—" he looked at Marta before momentarily linking his fingers with Sydney's and holding her hand up "—in these very capable hands." Before breaking the connection, he raised Sydney's hand to his lips and kissed it.

Annoyance pricked at Marta. She wasn't his to leave anywhere. Why did he just assume he could take possession of her, as if she were some wild strawberry growing in the field, waiting to be picked?

"Very considerate of you," she said coolly.

If she meant to put him off, she was going to have to do a lot better than that, he thought. Ike merely grinned, tickled by her tone. "Good thing I didn't take off my parka."

"Me, next!" Sara held up her hand to Ike to be kissed. She looked at Marta over her shoulder. "Did you know Ike's French?"

"I knew he was something," Marta murmured.

The laugh was low, unsettling. When Ike reached for her hand, Marta reflexively pulled it behind her back. He didn't press the matter. Instead, he inclined his head. "Nice meeting you, darlin'."

Marta raised her chin, a challenge in her eyes. "My name is Marta."

The grin grew wider, sexier. "Yes, I know, darlin'. I always pay attention, especially when there's a pretty woman involved."

Sydney moved between them again, escorting him the few steps to the front door. Afraid that Marta might say something to spoil her plans. She hooked her arm through Ike's. "Thanks for coming with me, Ike."

Genuine affection shone in his eyes when he looked at Sydney. "Always a pleasure spending time with you, you know that."

Impulse pushed an idea into Sydney's head. She'd planned on moving slowly, but maybe a full-scale attack would be the better way to go. After all, there were only two weeks with which to work.

"Come for dinner tonight. We're having your favorite."

The Kerrigan table already boasted of a dish he was interested in, Ike mused. "Don't go to any extra trouble for me. I'd come if you were serving shoe leather. It's the company, not the food, that I look forward to, darlin'. See you tonight." His eyes took in everyone in the room, resting fleetingly on Marta before he eased himself out the door.

Walking back to the all-terrain vehicle he'd left parked in the garage that he'd helped Shayne renovate six months ago, Ike began whistling softly. The wind stole the melody less than a couple of seconds after it emerged.

He glanced back over his shoulder, smiling. It looked as if things were going to be rather interesting for a little while.

If nothing else, Marta Jensen was certainly very easy on the eye. Seeing her without her parka had only confirmed his suspicions. Beneath it was a petite lady, small-boned and graceful—her wobbly descent from the airplane notwithstanding.

He'd watched her at the airport. There was a certain confidence in her walk, a certain tantalizing rhythm to the way her hips moved. The fact that she regarded him with a wide margin of suspicion and a heavy dose of wariness only made the pot at the end of the game that much more tempting to win.

He loved winning, but more than that, he loved a good challenge. And he loved a woman with a mind. There was no question that Marta Jensen was both.

Yes, indeed, it looked as if the next couple of weeks were going to be highly enjoyable.

The moment she met him, Marta knew why Sydney had elected to remain in Hades even after she'd discovered that the man she'd flown out to marry had run off with his ex-fiancé the day before she'd arrived. Tall, dark and handsome to a fault, Dr. Shayne Kerrigan looked like every woman's dream. Even better, he exuded strength and intelligence, Marta thought. He was capable of listening without flattering.

But the man Marta now found herself sitting across from at Sydney's dining room table was the antithesis of Shayne Kerrigan.

Well, maybe not quite. Both men were exceedingly good-looking, although in Ike's case the face was more rugged, the physique more muscular. Ike, according to the information Sydney had insisted on providing, had worked with his hands, and his mind, in one capacity or another from a very early age.

Right now, all she was aware of was that each time she looked in his direction—not at him, mind you, just in his direction—he was looking at her. Looking at her as if she were something rare and special he'd had the good fortune to stumble across.

Perhaps once, her head would have been turned and she might even have been smitten with him. Certainly she would have been flattered by the dark, sexy appraisal and the seductive smile that curved his generous mouth. But that was then.

And this was now.

If pressed, she would have admitted that his eyes, deep and brown, reminded her of a hot cup of coffee with just a hint of cream in it. A hot cup of coffee on a very cold winter's night.

Even if Sydney had never said a word about him to her, Marta would have surmised Ike LeBlanc had a string of conquests from here to the tip of the lower forty-nine. He just had that way about him.

On the surface, there was nothing not to like. If Shayne Kerrigan was the strong, silent type, his best friend was the strong, vocal type. And granted, it was not annoyingly vocal. Ike didn't talk on and on, overwhelming the listener. But it was how he said things, more than how often or how much. He could make "Please pass the salt" sound like the opening line to an invitation for a torrid night of lovemaking.

Marta knew all about men who were quick to smile, quick to murmur terms of endearment and undermine a woman's defenses. Knew all about men whose eyes led to the bedroom and whose words led to heartbreak.

She'd been, lamentably, a slow study, but she'd finally learned her lesson. Once was enough, thank you very much. She didn't believe in making the same mistake twice. Only fools did that.

Even so, it was hard not to find the man charming. Marta wished that Sydney hadn't placed Ike directly in her line of vision.

Luckily, the conversation all through dinner was almost nonstop, not a little of it thanks to Sara and Mac. Any momentary lull, however natural, was quickly filled with the sound of childish voices, asking Marta more questions, telling Ike what they'd done since his last visit to their table, sharing all their thoughts openly. Marta sat back and absorbed the atmosphere that vibrated around her, while trying to block out Ike's section of the table.

"You really struck gold up here," Marta enthused a little later as she helped Sydney get the dessert plates from the kitchen cupboard.

"We're the ones who struck gold," Shayne corrected Marta, walking into the room bearing a couple of plates. "Before Sydney came into our lives, Mac and Sara had set up hostile camps in the house. They wouldn't even talk to me. And, in their defense, I wasn't much of a father. I didn't know how to be one." There was love in his eyes when he looked at his wife. "It took Sydney to bring out the best in all of us."

Looking back, it was hard for Shayne to believe that all that was a little more than one short year in the past. After a six-year separation following a particularly bitter divorce, he'd suddenly found himself being called on to be a father again. His ex-wife had been killed in a car crash. With her gone, there was no longer anyone to stand in the way of his seeing his children, something she had done just to spite him. He'd brought them back from New York City, uprooting their lives and garnering only resentment as a harvest. When he'd brought Sydney into his home, giving her what he'd thought at the time was only temporary shelter, she'd walked straight into an armed camp.

Standing at her side, Shayne enveloped Sydney in his arms.

"She worked her magic on us and suddenly made us all realize how precious life was and how sinful it was to waste even a minute of it alone." Standing beside her, he kissed her temple. And even from that position, he felt the baby kick. Surprised, he laughed. "Looks like we're not going to be alone for a good, long time."

Marta could have sworn there was a twinkle in Sydney's eyes as she looked up at her husband.

"Oh, I think we can manage to find an island of time here and there." She glanced behind Shayne. "Ike'll baby-sit, won't you, Ike?"

Caught off guard, Marta turned around to see that Ike was standing behind her. For a tall man, he moved extremely quietly.

Bringing in more empty dinner plates, Ike placed them beside the sink. Clearly amused, he shook his head. "Now, you know I'll do anything for you, but watchin' a newborn's a little out of my league. Best you get one of the women from the village to tend to him or her until they're old enough to go ice fishing with me like those two in there." He nodded toward the dining room.

Well, at least there was something he didn't pretend he knew how to do, Marta thought, surprised at the disclaimer. She'd expected him to boast about his child-rearing abilities.

She supposed that wasn't being fair. She hadn't heard him actually boast about his abilities and accomplishments, real or imagined, the way Alex used to.

Still, she'd only been in Ike's company for a couple of hours, she reminded herself. Maybe he was just on his best behavior right now, such as it was.

As if on cue, Ike turned toward her, his eyes passing over her face like a gentle caress. "I'm actually at my best when the person I'm minding is far older than an infant.''

"That, I'm sure—'' Marta purposely made her tone sugary ''—is a matter of opinion.'' Picking up the pile of plates from the counter where Sydney had placed them, Marta turned her back to Ike and crossed back into the other room.

Shayne couldn't resist nudging Ike, his friend since elementary school. "Looks like you've got your work cut out with that one.''

"I've always loved a challenge, haven't you?'' Ike winked, taking the apple pie that he'd brought to dinner out of Sydney's hands. Using his back, he eased the door open and walked into the dining area.

Shayne looked down at Sydney. "He means it, you know.''

Sydney smiled warmly. "I know.''

"Maybe you better warn your friend.''

Sydney wasn't sure if *warn* was exactly the word to use here. She knew Ike to be a warm, caring human being. Not one woman who had ever shared his company had a single bad word to say about him. He left women better than he'd found them, with a renewed sense of confidence and a radiance about them. If nothing else, she wanted that for Marta. After what she'd gone through with Alex, she more than deserved it.

"Marta can take care of herself. Besides—'' Sydney smiled, looking at the closed door leading into the next room "—Ike might be the very best thing to happen to her in a long time.''

Chapter Four

The sound of the flames licking their way through the thick logs nestled in the dark brick hearth worked its way into the stillness of the room.

Holding the black mug of even blacker coffee between his hands, Ike sat back on the brandy-colored leather sofa, quietly regarding the woman who sat on the opposite end. She looked like an arrow poised to be released at any moment.

He wondered if he made her nervous. He was going to work on that. The prospect made him smile.

"You know who you remind me of?"

His deep voice, wedging into what had been a long silence, startled her. Marta took a breath, bracing herself. Oh, boy, here it came, the line he undoubtedly prized above all others. He was probably going to compare her to some bright, nubile young super-model currently reigning on the covers of fashion magazines, thinking that would make her pliant and receptive to his every suggestion.

Prepare to be disappointed, LeBlanc.

She turned haughty green eyes in his direction, confident she had his number. More confident that she wouldn't be dialing it. "Who?"

He smiled over the rim of his mug before taking a sip. "My sister, Juneau."

Marta stared at him. That wouldn't even have come close to making her list of flattering observations. Men who wanted to get a woman into their beds didn't make those kinds of comparisons. Just where did this backwater Lothario think he was going with this?

Her hands tightened around the mug of coffee she wasn't drinking. They were lingering over deep, robust coffee whose very aroma was guaranteed to keep a person awake throughout the six month night. Sitting before a roaring fire, for the moment they were alone. Shayne was in the tiny room that served as his study, talking to a distraught mother on the phone. Sydney had gone upstairs to tuck the children in, hopefully for the last time. They'd already come down twice, far more eager to share adult conversation than to put their heads down for the night on a pillow.

She didn't want to be alone with him.

Marta'd felt Ike's eyes skimming along her profile these last few minutes and had been bracing herself for the mother of all come-ons.

Comparing her to his sister wasn't exactly what she would have labeled as a come-on. Her eyes narrowed. "Do I look like her?"

Ike laughed softly under his breath. His sister had long, straight black hair the color of midnight, not short, riotous locks that rivaled the flames in the fireplace. Taking after their mother's side of the family, Junie's skin was a hint darker than his, and her eyes were almost black.

"God, no. Junie's almost as tall as I am and as thin as a whaler's harpoon. At least she was," he amended more soberly, "the last time I saw her."

It'd been three years since June had taken off. Three years since he'd found the note on the bar saying that she was finally getting out of this deep-freeze. It had come on the heels of an argument, and ended with a warning: *Please don't come looking for me, just be happy for me.*

As if he could be happy, not knowing where she was. Unbeknownst to her, he'd tracked her down. But she'd seemed happy, so he had done the only thing he could. He had honored her wishes and blamed himself for not having made it easier for her to leave. But she'd been so young when she'd voiced her displeasure, and he'd thought it was just a phase. Hindsight showed him that he'd been selfish, but when he'd attempted to tell her so in a letter a year ago, it had been returned Addressee Unknown. She'd moved on.

He prayed she was happy.

His eyes washed over Marta before he continued. "While you're a little bit of a thing with a nice share of curves."

Marta pressed her lips together, ready to fend off what more was coming in the wake of those words. He'd just made a slow start with the comparison, that's all. But he was coming to the snow job now.

With her back against the arm of the sofa, she regarded him coolly. "If we're so different, why do I remind you of your sister?"

"It's that look in your eyes when we talk about Hades." He paused, taking another sip. Taking his time. There was no reason to hurry. Life had a completely different pace here than in the other states. Here the steps were unhurried, well-placed. "Junie had the same look in her eyes. She was restless here, dying to get out."

Marta could understand why. She still couldn't quite come to terms with the fact that Sydney appeared to be happy living out here. "And I take it she got out."

"Yes." Ike looked into his mug, watching the firelight shimmer along the inky surface. "She did."

Was he going to tell her now that he missed his sister? Missed female companionship? Marta grew tense, waiting for the shoe to drop. "Where did she go?"

He shrugged, draining his cup and setting it down on the coffee table. He didn't feel like going into details, into defending actions he now felt were in-defensible. When the letter had been returned, he'd tried to find her and had discovered she'd purposely hidden her trail. That had hurt.

"Beats me."

Her eyes narrowed to emerald pinpoints. "You don't know?"

Ike heard the accusation in her voice, the emo-tion, and wondered what was behind it. Sitting back, he crossed one booted foot over his thigh. He gave her the short, public version. "She didn't want me to know. Junie ran off with her boyfriend. A guy who thought he was going to take the music world by storm, strumming his guitar and singing songs nobody understood."

The laugh was short, without his customary hu-mor behind it. Roy Watkins, son of an oil man who had just been passing through, was one of the few human beings he'd ever encountered that he hadn't liked, even a little. How much of that was justified and how much was because he was Junie's big brother? He couldn't honestly say.

"But Junie thought the world began and ended in his shadow, so that's where she wanted to be." He looked into the fire, remembering. Blocking the anger the memory stirred. "Roy's shadow was go-ing out of here, and that was just fine with her. Ever since she'd been a little girl, all she ever talked about was getting on the other side of the northern lights." Ike turned his eyes toward Marta. "One day, they both just took off together."

"There are ways to find people."

Ike inclined his head, acknowledging her point but adding one of his own. "If they want to be found."

That shouldn't have anything to do with it, Marta thought in disgust. Juneau was his sister, he was supposed to maintain ties—not write her off as if she hadn't existed. Or be glad she was gone because she'd been too much trouble.

Like Marta had been for the mother who had so cavalierly given her up because the child got in the way of having a good time. Marta banked down the thought and the faded memory it aroused.

Don't leave me, Mama. Don't leave me here.

But the door had slammed anyway, and the social worker had led her away. She'd been five at the time. Five years old when she'd become part of The System.

Marta's eyes looked pointedly into his. "Even if they don't."

There was something going on there behind her eyes, Ike thought. Something that bore exploring. But not quite yet. First, he had to gain her confidence. "People are entitled to privacy if they want it. I figured Junie wanted it. If she hadn't, she would have gotten in contact with me." Not tried to remain hidden, he added silently.

"That's kind of a lazy approach, isn't it?"

Well, she didn't pull her punches, he'd give her that. There was something to be admired about a woman who was so honest. Holding his hand out, palm up, he suddenly closed his fingers as if he was grasping something. ''You hold onto a bird too tight, you kill it.'' And above all, he wanted June to feel free and happy.

Marta frowned at the analogy. ''There's such a thing as a happy medium.''

''Junie didn't want a happy medium. She wanted something new, exciting. She knows where to find me if she ever needs anything.''

And it was his fond hope that someday, his sister would choose to contact him one way or another. Even after all this time, he sorely missed her. Missed the bond they'd once shared.

Spoken like a man who really doesn't care, Marta thought. If she'd had a sister, she would have done whatever she could to keep her in her life. ''Maybe she's too proud to ask, did you ever think of that?''

He had, but he couldn't quite get himself to believe that of Junie. ''Pride's for other people, not for family.'' His sister knew he wasn't the type to rub her nose in a mistake, no matter how great. All he wanted was her happiness.

Ike wondered if she'd found it with Roy.

Marta shrugged, looking away. *Family.* The single word still shimmered like a mystery, the solution just out of reach. ''I wouldn't know about that.''

Ike knew a little about her. About the foster homes. Sydney had told him. ''There's family and then there's family.''

She slanted a look at him. ''Meaning?''

There was something in her eyes, something he doubted she was even aware of, that made him want to gather her into his arms and tell her things were going to be all right—even though he had no idea what those things might be.

"There's the family you're born into, and the one you make for yourself."

She wasn't sure she was following him. "You mean marriage?"

If that's what he meant, she thought it a rather strange reference, given what Sydney had told her about Ike. She would have thought the institution of marriage to be so far from his thoughts that he couldn't reach it by plane.

Ike acknowledged her response, but he'd been thinking along different lines. "Or just friends. Like you are with Sydney. She said you two were closer than most sisters."

The observation made Marta smile. "Yes, I suppose we are."

Was it her imagination, or was he sitting closer to her now than he had been a moment before? She glanced down at her own seat and realized that, somehow, she had been the one to move, not him. How had that happened? She pressed her back into the cushions of the sofa, determined to remain exactly where she was and not move an inch closer.

"And yet you tried to talk her out of coming here." Watching her, Ike tried to hide his amusement. Did she think he was going to pounce on her?

"I did."

He heard the defensiveness in her voice. Obviously she thought he was going to tell her she was wrong. Though he loved the town he'd been born in, Ike was more than capable of looking at the situation from her point of view. "I would have done the same thing in your place." He saw the surprise that came into her eyes. He rather liked the fact that he wasn't living up—or down—to her expectations. "Not an easy thing—pulling up stakes and moving to somewhere you've only read about. Takes a lot of guts."

Leaning forward, he picked up the framed photograph on the coffee table, studying it for a moment. It was taken the day Sydney and Shayne were married. He remembered that it was a quick, impromptu ceremony. There'd hardly been enough time to find an appropriate dress for Sydney. She made a beautiful bride. And she made Shayne happier than Ike had ever remembered seeing his friend.

"Hell of a woman, Sydney."

He'd get no argument from her on that. Marta dearly loved Sydney. That was why she was surprised that part of her was almost envious of the admiration she heard in Ike's voice. It was an old feeling, rising up from the past. A feeling that had once made her want to say, "Me, too. Notice me, too." A feeling she'd carried with her through all the different foster homes she'd lived in over the years. A feeling that she'd harbored as she'd secretly watched the foster mother or father she'd been assigned to talk to their son or daughter.

Even the nicest of them had spoken differently to her than they had to their own child. She knew that they might not have meant to make a distinction, but she'd always heard it anyway. She was receiving kindness, sympathy, pity, while their own child received love.

It made all the difference in the world to her.

Rousing herself, she saw that Ike had set the frame down on the table again and was looking at her.

"Yes, she is," she agreed. "One hell of a woman. I could never do that, come out here to live." She glanced toward the window. There was only darkness outside. No streetlights, nothing. "It's too lonely."

Ike looked at her thoughtfully. "Doesn't have to be. Loneliness is something a person carries around inside them. You can be lonely in a crowd. Me, I figure there're more lonely people in places like New York and Los Angeles than there are in Hades. One person's loneliness is another person's peacefulness. It's all in how you see things."

When he looked into her eyes like that, she felt he was looking right into her. She shifted. He was hitting a little too close to home. "Are you the town philosopher?"

He laughed. That honor belonged to Billy Wilcox. He could philosophize the socks right off you, as long as you kept the beers coming.

"No, the saloon keeper. Comes with the territory, darlin'." The wicked smile mellowed into something just a tad less unsettling. "Besides, I like helping people with their problems."

Marta doubted anyone would be canonizing him anytime soon. "Or creating them. Sydney's told me all about you."

There was pleasure, rather than embarrassment, in his eyes. "You asked. I'm touched."

The last thing she wanted was for him to get the wrong idea. She wasn't about to be fair game for him. "Don't be. I didn't. She volunteered."

Shifting, he moved just a little closer to her without appearing to move at all. "She couldn't have told it right."

Why was it, when he looked at her, she felt like a skater trying to make it across a stretch of very thin ice? "Why's that?"

His eyes smiled into hers. "Because you've decided not to like me."

She wished that he'd stop whatever it was he was doing to make her fidget inside. "I don't intend to have any feelings at all about you."

"Everybody's got feelings about everything that's around them. That's how choices get made. You pick the light toast over the dark." He touched the cup she still clutched in her hands. "Coffee over tea." His eyes holding hers, he flicked a finger over her arm. "A sweater over a blouse."

She felt her breath catch in her throat. The room had suddenly become a great deal warmer than it had been a moment earlier. Warmer and smaller. "Doesn't mean I'll sleep with them," she blurted without thinking.

His smile seemed to burrow deep within her. "Nobody said anything about sleeping."

She realized that she'd blurted the words out without thinking.

Okay, you're good, I'll give you that. Now back off. Marta held herself very stiffly as she looked at him.

"Sydney said you've slept with most of the women in the area."

Very slowly, he shook his head. "Those weren't Sydney's words." He looked at her knowingly. "What she probably said is that I've made love with most of the women in the area."

He admitted it. Not even Alex had done that when she'd confronted him. Didn't the man have any sense of decency at all? "Same difference."

He caught her arm as she began to rise from the sofa. Despite the accusing look in her eyes, Ike left his hand where it was, forcing her to remain seated.

"Not in my book. There're a lot of ways to make love, darlin'."

Marta gave him a withering look. "Please, spare me."

The put-down only made his grin deepen. "I'll remember you said that. But as to what I was saying, you can make love with a woman by talking, by touching." He took the cup gently from her hands, noting with satisfaction that her fingers had grown just the slightest bit lax. "By looking." His eyes caressed her face. "By sharing a thought. Doesn't have to mean sharing a body. That's the last part of it. A lovely part, but the rest of it's just as satisfying in its own way."

There seemed to be no room between them at all. How had he managed that? Marta hadn't seen him move. If she didn't know any better, she would have said that she was the victim of some sort of hypnosis. And it was his voice, not just his eyes, that were casting a spell. But it was one she was determined not to succumb to.

Blinking didn't seem to help.

"Sometimes even more so. It's a matter of preference. Me, I love all women. Love the scent of them, the sound of their laughter. Love making them smile, especially when they feel sad." And this woman, Ike thought, had had a great deal of sadness in her life. He'd have to ask Sydney for answers. But for now, he supposed that made them kindred spirits, in a way. "What makes you smile, darlin'?"

Marta's pulse was scrambling like a mouse fleeing a pursuing cat on slippery terrain. Mystified, she saw that her hands had somehow gotten into his. She drew them back abruptly.

"Hearing my name said instead of a term you can attach indiscriminately because you can't remember who you're talking to."

Ike knew she probably wouldn't react well to being told she looked cute when she was angry. But that didn't change the fact that she did. "I always know who I'm talking to. Most women like being called darlin'." His eyes shifted to someone behind her. "Don't you, darlin'?"

Marta turned, expecting to see Sydney standing there. But instead, it was Sara who was behind her. But only for a moment. The next, the little girl was launching herself into Ike's arms like a human baseball. He barely had enough time to make the catch.

"Save me!" she cried dramatically.

Sydney entered the room half a beat behind her daughter. At the sight of her, sympathy nudged at Ike. Sydney looked beyond tired. It was a good thing Marta had come when she had. Sydney could use the help.

His arms closed around the pint-size torpedo and he nuzzled her.

"Save you from what? The big, bad mommy? Sorry, but she might wallop me if I get between you and your bedtime." Still holding her, he turned Sara around so that she faced him. "Don't you know that going to bed on time'll make you grow up to be as beautiful looking as your momma?"

Sara's eyes grew wide as she looked at him in genuine wonder and utter disbelief. "It will?"

His face serious, Ike crossed his heart, then held up his hand as if he were taking a solemn oath.

"I'd never lie to you, darlin'." And then the same smile appeared. It was easy to see that the little girl was smitten with him. "You know that."

She nodded her head, looking as solemn as he

did. "Yes, I do." Turning, she began to march out of the room.

"And just where do you think you're off to?" Sydney called after her.

"To bed, Mommy." With that, Sara hurried to the stairs.

Bemused, Sydney looked at Ike.

He crossed to her to save her the steps. It was time he was leaving anyway. "She just came down to say she won't be coming down anymore."

"This had better be the last time, Sara," Sydney told her. Going up and down the stairs was getting to be a real chore for her.

"Oh, it is," Sara promised. "I want to be beautiful, like you."

Sydney saw no connection. She looked over her shoulder at Ike, knowing he had to have something to do with the mystifying message. He merely winked at her and grinned.

"I'd better be going. The dinner, as always, was delicious. Anytime you want a new job as a cook at the Salty, just say the word." He kissed Sydney's cheek affectionately. "And tell that big lug of yours good-night for me—if he ever gets off the telephone."

"It's Mrs. McGuire on the phone," Sydney told him.

The light dawned. "Well, that explains it." He could see by the confusion on Marta's face that she had no idea what they were talking about. Apparently Sydney had filled her in on the local color rather selectively. "As a rule, Mrs. McGuire likes to talk people's ears off. Shayne's just too polite to hang up on her. She's got nine kids and there's usually something wrong with at least one of them." Taking his parka from the hook, Ike slipped his arms into the sleeves. "Any news about his getting any help out here?"

Sydney shook her head, sighing. "They're still trying to find someone to come out, at least a nurse practitioner, if not a doctor. But there's not exactly a stampede from the newly minted medical community to Hades."

"Maybe if you changed the name of the town," Marta suggested. "It might be a minor thing, but you have to admit the town's name is pretty off-putting."

Ike tucked his scarf into the parka before zipping it up. "Then you'd have to come up with a whole new legend on how the town was named."

Marta looked at Sydney quizzically. "There's a legend?"

"You do the honors," Sydney said to Ike. "You tell it so much better than I can."

"Old stories become legends after a time," Ike began. "Hades was settled by a couple of miners who'd come here—part of the rush looking for gold. They'd stayed, trying to get lucky, until they ran out of money and didn't even have enough to book passage home again, wherever that was."

He slipped on his gloves. "So, with no money and no choice, they decided to make a home for themselves right here. One of them was said to remark that the only thing worse than being here was being in Hades, and the other said that this *was* Hades, just without the heat. Anytime someone else down on his luck came into town and asked where they were, one of the two prospectors would say, 'In Hades.' The name stuck after a while.''

"That's a good story, Ike." They all looked up the stairs to see that Sara had gotten no farther than the landing, and was now peering down at them through the slats. She was looking at Ike hopefully. "Tell me another one."

He took the stairs two at a time until he was beside her. Getting down on one knee, he kissed Sara's cheek, much the way he had her mother's, then took her by the shoulders and turned her around until she was facing her room.

"Next time I'm here. That's a promise, darlin'. Now go get beautiful for me."

Covering her mouth with both hands, Sara giggled and ran off.

He probably got all the women to do his bidding that way, Marta thought. "Charm" was something you had to work to build up an immunity to.

Sydney watched as he came down the stairs again. "I should have you over for dinner every night."

Ready to leave again, Ike laughed. "Don't have to twist my arm, darlin', though I think Shayne might have something to say about that after a while. I'll see you good people later." His hand on the doorknob, Ike lingered a moment, looking at Marta. "Have you given my showing you around the area any more thought?"

"No." Marta had been too busy unpacking and then helping Sydney with dinner to think about it at all. "But like I said, I'm not here to play tourist."

"But you do have to play sometime, darlin'. You know what they say, all work and no play—"

"—leaves a woman intact for another day," she countered.

"I do like you, Marta Jensen. I surely do." Then, just before he pulled open the door, he kissed her cheek quickly. He was gone before she could utter a word of protest.

It wasn't until she turned around to face Sydney that Marta realized he'd finally used her name.

Chapter Five

The wind sounded a little mournful, Ike mused, thinking of his conversation with Marta as he carefully watched the road. He knew every square inch of the land the way a young lover knew every part of his first love's body, but on a night like this, it was still easy to take a wrong turn. And end up frozen by morning.

By the time he made it back to the Salty Saloon, Ike had long since stopped feeling his toes and his legs and arms were in jeopardy of going numb. It was a cold night, even by the standards he was accustomed to.

It was the kind of night, he mused, throwing the switch that opened the door to his heated garage, that made a man long to have a woman beside him to keep him warm. And to help keep warm.

He smiled to himself, thinking of Marta. Now there was a woman who looked very capable of warming a man's blood. He certainly wouldn't mind trying to keep her warm. And, after a bit, he doubted that she would have any objections.

What would it take to make Marta thaw out? To make her stop being suspicious of him, just lean back and let things happen naturally?

Ike was looking forward to finding out, he thought as he walked from the garage to the back entrance of the bar. His cheeks stung from the wind as he reached the back door. The lights from the Salty were all on, casting dim beams that burrowed their way into the snow.

How many brave souls had pitted themselves against the elements to come out and share a drink with a few acquaintances when they could just as easily have the same drinks with a great deal less trouble at home?

He smiled. The allure of gathering in a communal hall with friends was hard to resist, thank God. Otherwise, his first business venture might have proven to be his last. The Salty was the only establishment catering to the social needs of the people in and around Hades. It wasn't unusual, when the weather was particularly nasty, for his patrons to spend the night sacked out on the floor. It went part and parcel with the philosophy behind running the Salty. You gave a man more than just a glass of ale when he came in, you gave him your friendship.

If once in a while that included giving him a place to spend the night, that was fine, too.

Ike nodded at a few of the regulars as he entered the bar, returning their greetings as he stomped the snow from the bottom of his boots. There were about twenty men scattered throughout the room and two more in the back, arguing over a pool table. He was within his rights to close up, but he hadn't the heart. Besides, home was just a flight of stairs away, now that he lived over the bar.

Hanging up his parka on the rack just beneath the antiquated moose head that the previous owner had thrown in when he'd sold the Salty to him, Ike made his way over to the bar. Jean Luc was at the far end, setting another tall one in front of Shawn McGuire. There were times when they would have sworn the man was hollow.

His cousin was as fair as Ike was dark. It was hard to believe that their fathers were brothers and that they shared the same French grandmother. But while Ike's mother had been one-third Inuit, one-third Native American and one-third black Irish, Luc's mother had come from Sweden, and he had taken his blond hair and blue eyes from her. At times, it made Luc look younger than he was, evoking almost a paternal feeling from Ike, despite the fact that they were separated by only three years.

Luc looked a little tired to him as Ike drew closer. He reached for the permanently stained half apron and tied it carelessly about his waist.

"Why don't you go on up to bed? I'll take over.

I'm too wired to sleep, anyway.'' The way he felt right now, Ike thought, he'd probably be able to stay up around the clock. It wouldn't be the first time.

Though Luc had been serving McGuire when Ike crossed to him, his eyes had been fixed on the occupant of the booth in the rear. He shifted them now to Ike. He'd been waiting for Ike to return for the last half hour.

''There's a lady here to see you. She's been waiting for a while now.''

Ike took McGuire's money and rang up the sale. The old-fashioned cash register sounded melodic as its drawer opened. He hadn't noticed a woman in the bar. ''Pretty?''

Luc glanced toward the rear again. The booth was still occupied. ''I don't think that's going to matter this time, Ike.''

Ike laughed softly, rubbing away a ring of moisture on the counter. ''It always matters, boy. To the lady, if not to anyone else.'' He paused, the dish towel still in his hand. Luc was acting strangely. Women frequented the Salty all the time. ''What's the matter?''

Rather than answer, Luc motioned him over to the other end of the bar. From there, Ike could see her. She was sitting alone, swaddled in a heavy gray parka that was partially unzipped. A scarf lay on the table beside her. She wasn't having anything to drink. The face was unfamiliar to him.

''Did you tell her the first one's on the house?''

Luc shook his head. "She didn't come here to drink, Ike."

There was something in Luc's voice that made him a little uneasy, though for the life of him, Ike wouldn't have been able to say why. "Then why did she come?"

Luc had no answer. "She said she'd only talk to you."

"Well, then I'd better go see her." Tossing the towel aside, Ike rounded the bar and crossed over to the small booth at the rear of the room.

He was less than two feet away when he finally realized that the stranger, a woman he judged to be in her mid-twenties, wasn't alone. She had a baby sleeping in a basket on the seat beside her.

He curtailed an impulse to upbraid her. It wasn't his place to tell her what to do, but what would possess a woman to venture out on a night like this with an infant? Ike wasn't so divorced from his own upbringing that he didn't know the answer to that one. *Hard times.* Maybe she was down on her luck and looking for a place to stay. The only thing that passed as a hotel in Hades was boarded up for the season. It wasn't profitable to keep it open in the dead of winter. The quarters upstairs over the Salty were small by some standards, especially since he and Luc shared them, but he figured that something could be arranged for the night.

In the morning, he'd see if there was someone in the area who could take her in until she got on her feet. In hardship cases, Reverend Hathaway and his wife were usually good for a week or two.

The entire thought process had taken only a split second. Just long enough for Ike to reach her booth.

The woman looked tired, stressed. The smile he offered her was one of sympathy as he leaned over her table. "Is there something I can get you?"

"Are you Klondyke?" Even as she asked, a look of relief began to take over her features.

"Yes, ma'am." He inclined his head, then peered a little more closely at her. "Do I know you?" He knew he didn't. It was his gift never to forget a face, and this one had never crossed his path before.

"No." The woman shook her head. "She said you'd be tall. And that you had the kindest eyes she'd ever seen." She struggled to remember, to get the wording just right. It was important. "When there wasn't a wicked gleam in them."

Well, that certainly didn't narrow the playing field. The observation could have come from a lot of women. "I'm afraid you have the advantage, Miss—"

"Ruth," the woman said quickly. "Ruth Jackson."

Like the face, the name meant nothing to him. "If you don't mind me asking, should you have brought your baby here?"

"I didn't bring my baby," she corrected. "I brought yours."

Was she going to claim that the sleeping infant

was the result of some torrid night he didn't remember? He was willing to take an oath that he had never touched her. Even more than the faces of his customers, Ike remembered the face of every woman he had ever made love with. And she was not among them.

Ike shook his head, trying to respond as delicately as possible. "I don't—"

He never got the chance. Ruth moved forward, her hand on the basket to keep it from falling. "Her name is Celine. Celine LeBlanc. Your sister named her after your mother."

The mention of his sister had him looking around, half expecting to see her step out of the shadows. "Junie? This is Junie's baby?" The woman nodded.

He could hardly believe it. His little sister had a baby. Closer scrutiny had him seeing Junie's mouth, her cheekbones and her dark hair. "Where is she? Why didn't she come herself?"

"She can't." Ruth hesitated. She seemed nervous, sympathetic, as she placed a hand over his. "Mr. LeBlanc, I really don't know how to say this to you, but—"

She didn't have to tell him. The moment he saw the look in Ruth's eyes, he knew. Knew beyond a shadow of a doubt. They'd said his great-grandmother on his mother's side had been a seer, and a hint of the gift occasionally came over him. As it did now.

The pain was staggering, robbing him of his

breath, pressing so heavily on his chest that he felt himself go numb from head to foot. His heart froze mid-beat. His little sister was dead.

"How?"

"There were complications during the birth. Internal bleeding. They thought they got it all, but…" Ruth sighed. "She died a week after having Celine. I came to see her in the hospital. She asked me to bring the baby to you if anything happened." Ruth looked over to the sleeping baby. "Said you'd take care of Celine the way you had her."

His expression was stony as he struggled with the shock. "If I'd taken care of her, she'd be here telling me about the baby herself, instead of you."

There was compassion in Ruth's eyes. "June said you'd blame yourself. She told me to tell you not to. That she knew what she was doing, or thought she did."

When you're eighteen, you feel you have all the answers. There hadn't been any way to stop her. But he should have. He should have found a way. "Who's the father?"

"Roy Watkins."

The name made him curl his fingers into his hands, wishing he could have wrapped them around the boy's throat instead. If it hadn't been for Roy, Junie wouldn't have run off. She would never have left by herself, and maybe, in time, she would have chosen to stay.

"Where is he?"

Ruth shook her head. "Nobody knows. He took

off right after June told him she was pregnant.'' She
must have seen the question in his eyes. "She was
too proud to come home and ask for your help. She
wanted to make it on her own. She would have,
too,'' Ruth added loyally, "except that she just
wasn't strong enough.''

The baby stirred, making a small sound in her
sleep. Snaring his attention. "How far did she
get?''

"Excuse me?''

He looked at the young woman again. "June
wanted to get as far away from this place as she
could.'' Like so many others here, she'd talked in-
cessantly of going to Los Angeles or New York, or
somewhere equally as exciting and thriving. "How
far did she get?''

"Fairbanks. That's where he left her. We both
worked at the makeup counter in Wilcox department store.'' There was fondness in Ruth's voice.
"She was a good person.''

"Yes, I know that,'' he answered quietly. Emotion choked him as he came around to stand beside
the baby. Celine was sleeping despite the din in the
bar.

A baby. His baby sister had had a baby. Even
looking at the infant, it just didn't seem possible.
He raised his eyes to Ruth, forcing himself to function. "Have you got a place to stay tonight?''

She nodded. "I made arrangements before I
came. One of my uncles went to the seminary with
a friend of your minister. I'm staying with them

until morning. I have to be getting back to my job,''
she apologized.

As if to back up her words, the door to the Salty
opened and the minister's eldest son, Conrad,
walked in. Seeing him, Ruth rose from the table.
She hesitated a moment before leaving. ''If you'd
like, I could keep Celine until morning…''

For one brief moment, he was tempted to let her.
Tempted to keep this painful reminder of his sister's
demise out of his sight for as long as he possibly
could. But denying Celine's existence wouldn't
bring Junie back.

''You've already done more than enough, Ruth.''
He began to pick up the basket, then stopped.
''Who took care of the funeral arrangements?''

''June had a little money put by. Enough to cover
a cremation. I scattered her ashes when the wind
was blowing east. It's where she was heading.''

''Thank you.'' It was fitting, he supposed. At
least a part of Junie would wind up being where
she'd wanted to go. But that left him without even
a grave site to visit. He felt cheated somehow. In a
way, it was as if his sister had never existed, except
in his mind.

A small noise, louder this time than before,
caught his attention. He wouldn't need a grave to
remind him of his sister. He had Celine.

Grief hammered at Ike's soul, trying to break
down the barriers he was so hastily constructing all
around him. The moment the woman left, giving

him the bag filled with formula she'd brought with her and agreeing to see him again before she left Hades, he'd thrown himself into preparations to make conditions livable for Celine. He deliberately rejected Luc's offer to help, ignored the handful of questions that came his way as he crossed the floor of the bar with Celine, and went upstairs to try to pull something together.

The thing he most needed to pull together, himself, he ignored. Ike figured putting one foot before the other would take care of that eventually. He just had to remember to keep moving.

He still didn't believe this was happening. Surely, he would wake up tomorrow morning to discover that Junie was still alive and that this had all just been a very bad dream.

As if reading his mind, Celine gurgled from her basket on the floor beside the bed, kicking to free her trapped legs from beneath the layers of blanket tucked around her. Sitting on the edge of the bed, his face in his hands, he looked down at her.

"Don't start struggling. That's how your momma started out, struggling to be free. And look where it got her."

He took a deep breath, letting it out slowly. Trying to gather his scattered thoughts together. Trying to send his scattered emotions away.

Celine started to cry.

"Oh, now, don't do that, little one. I'll take care of you." Very gently, he picked up the baby. "I didn't mean to make you feel like you weren't wanted."

For a second, the whimpering died away. Celine's huge brown eyes seemed to delve right into him, as if she were absorbing the sound of his voice.

"You do look like her, you know. And you could do worse than grow up to be the spitting image of your momma." The whimpers returned as she began to gnaw on her tiny fist. "Oh, now, don't cry again. I didn't mean you wouldn't be your own person. I just...I just..." He could feel his own tears starting. "Oh, hell." The word echoed in his head, making him ashamed. "I didn't mean that. I promise I won't swear once you're old enough to understand, but you're going to have to give me a little time to get used to this. A little time..."

He pressed his lips together. "She won't be coming home anymore, will she? She won't be coming back to either one of us." He felt the tears begin to slip down his face as he mourned the loss of a life too soon ended. Celine wriggled against him. "Nothing's ever going to hurt you, little one," he whispered to the baby. "I promise."

"Talk about your pioneer spirit," Marta said, standing in the kitchen doorway. The aroma of freshly brewed coffee drifted seductively through the bright room.

Surprised, Sydney turned around from the counter. "What are you doing up so early?"

Marta crossed to her and took quick inventory. There was a carton of eggs, a package of bacon, bread, waffle batter. It looked like a full-size breakfast to her. "I thought I'd surprise you with breakfast. Looks like I should have come down earlier."

Sydney opened the cupboard, looking for the frying pans. "Couldn't sleep, huh?" Sydney smiled at her, remembering. "I had trouble sleeping here, too, in the beginning. But you get used to it."

"I'm not planning on living that long." Marta began cracking eggs against the bowl, emptying them into it. "But you certainly seem to have gotten used to it." Although God only knows how. "You look very happy."

"That's because I am." Sydney drew the toaster closer to the work area. "I don't think I've ever been happier in my life. Shayne's a wonderful man, we're doing a lot of good out here, and the kids—well, you've seen the kids."

"Yes, they're great. And Shayne's great. You're all great," Marta pronounced, then looked at Sydney with a touch of wistfulness. "But couldn't you be just as great in, say, Omaha?"

Sydney placed her hand on Marta's shoulder. Leaving Marta behind had been the only thing she'd ever regretted about her move. "This is where Shayne belongs. And you know, I think I do, too. You build stronger ties here. People need one another here."

Marta pitched the last of the eggshells into the garbage.

"Yes, to form a human chain so they can get from one place to another when it snows." She bit her lower lip. Maybe she wasn't being fair. But it didn't seem fair that her friend was buried up here, either. "I just always thought we'd wind up taking some place by storm, I guess. Not having the storm take us—or in this case, you."

Touched, Sydney looked at Marta. "Be happy for me, Marta."

"I am. You know I am. I guess I just miss you, that's all. I guess I was hoping that maybe you'd exaggerated in your letters about being happy here. That you'd actually missed Omaha." One look at her in the airport had told Marta that her hopes were misplaced. "But you don't."

"No, I don't. Just you." Rummaging through the drawer, she found the wire whisk. Marta took it from her and began beating the eggs. "So tell me all about everyone at the school. Who did they get to take my place?"

Marta made herself comfortable on the stool as she continued beating the eggs. "Her name's Vera MacKenzie, and she's quite an adjustment after you—"

She stopped beating and listened. There *was* someone knocking on the door. It wasn't even 7:00 a.m. Marta looked at Sydney. "Visitors start coming early around here. Guess they can't stand the solitude, either."

"At this time in the morning, they're coming to

see the doctor, not looking for company.'' Sydney looked around for a dish towel to wipe her hands.

''Stay there, I can get it.'' Marta hopped off the stool.

''I used to be able to hop like that.''

Marta laughed. ''Your hopping days are just beginning.''

She looked down at her stomach. She felt as if she'd been pregnant forever. It was going to be a relief to finally have this over with, even if it meant a huge increase in activity on the home front. ''Don't I know it.''

The knock came again, this time more forcefully. Marta hurried the rest of the way to the door. She hoped she wouldn't see anything grizzly when she opened it. Some of Sydney's letters about the kind of injuries that were sustained in the wild had been pretty detailed.

Being cautious, she unlocked the door and then opened it only a crack. Ike was standing on the doorstep holding something against him. It was tightly wrapped and completely covered with what looked like someone's parka.

''A little early to be paying a social call, isn't it?'' She glanced at the bundle. Was it her eyes, or did the bundle just move? She opened the door farther to let him come in. A rush of cold wind followed him. She could feel gooseflesh forming all along her body. Marta quickly shut the door behind him. ''If I didn't know any better, I would say you have a baby with you.''

Ike looked around. Where was Sydney? "Then you would be right." Very carefully, trying not to be as awkward as he felt, Ike tossed aside the parka wrapper. A sound between a whimper and a sigh came from the tiny mouth. Huge brown eyes looked right at Marta.

Stunned, Marta stared first at the infant, then at Ike. "You have a baby?"

Ike made his way past her. Where *was* everyone? "I do now."

Chapter Six

"Ike, what brings you out so early in the—"

Lured from the kitchen by the sound of his voice, Sydney stopped dead as she entered the living room. Her eyes were wide and quizzical as she looked from the baby in Ike's arms to his face. She couldn't begin to read his expression, but the man who returned her gaze was not the Ike she knew.

"Ike?"

"It's Junie's." He looked down at the small bundle as if he'd forgotten he was carrying the infant and only the sound of Sydney's voice, intruding into his train of thought, had reminded him. "It's a girl."

The words fit awkwardly in Ike's mouth. He'd had all night to get used to the idea. To get used to

Celine's presence in his life. To the notion that she was his niece and now his to care for.

And he'd had all night to resist, with all his heart, the overwhelming, bitter knowledge that his sister was gone. That somehow Celine had traded places with Junie—that a child he hadn't known about existed, while the sister he'd loved did not.

He couldn't make his peace with that, with knowing that he'd never see Junie again, but that wasn't Sydney's problem. Only his.

Ike cleared his throat and held the baby up a little higher. His arms were beginning to ache. He'd held her most of the night—to still her crying, and the ache in his heart.

"Her name's Celine."

Cautiously, as if afraid of triggering something, Sydney moved closer. She looked down at the baby Ike held. A full shock of black hair graced the tiny head. She'd never met Juneau LeBlanc, but once Ike had shown her a worn photograph of his sister that he kept tucked away in his wallet.

The smile Sydney offered him was warm, comforting. Compassionate. "She looks just like her."

"Yeah." He exhaled the word, his arms unconsciously tightening around the baby. "She does."

Something in his tone alerted Sydney. She exchanged looks with Marta. Gently, Sydney placed a hand on his arm. "Ike, where's June?"

But he didn't answer. Instead, he moved so that Sydney was forced to drop her hand. Ike crossed to the bottom of the stairs, looking up.

"Where's Shayne? I want him to check the baby out. You know, make sure there's nothing wrong with her." Ike turned to see both women looking at him with something he didn't want to read in their eyes. He talked quickly, burying what he was feeling. "Isn't that what you're supposed to do with infants? Have them checked out? 'Something' baby care I think it's called."

"Well baby care," Marta supplied.

"Right. That." Celine whimpered against him as he turned abruptly back to the stairs and looked up again. "Is he still sleeping? I thought Shayne never slept."

Knowing that there was something horribly wrong, afraid to put it into words even in her own mind, Sydney moved toward the stairs. "I'll go get him."

Ike swallowed. Damn, was his throat ever going to stop feeling as if there were a boulder stuck in it? "Thanks."

Marta shook her head, coming next to him. Compassion tugged at her, but she knew firsthand that it was a mistake to offer it. It only made things worse. "You're holding her all wrong."

His brain still felt as if he were moving through a fog. Everything was so jumbled in his head, despite his struggling to sort it out. "What?"

Marta smoothed back the blanket tucked around the baby. Celine's head wasn't properly elevated, and she was making her discomfort known. "That's why she's crying. You're holding her all wrong."

Ike felt as if he were doing everything all wrong. Things were spinning out of control. "I don't have much practice at this."

That certainly would have been her guess, Marta thought. "I've had my share. Why don't you give her to me?" She didn't wait for his agreement, but started to take Celine from him even as she made the suggestion.

There was momentary resistance in his eyes, but then it receded. Ike surrendered Celine to her.

Even as a little girl, Marta had felt that there was something almost heavenly about holding an infant in her arms. A sweetness poured all through her, softening her heart. "There now, sugar," she cooed to the baby, smiling at Celine. "It's okay. Nobody's going to drop you anymore."

A touch of indignation was roused at what Ike took to be a not-so-veiled put-down. "I didn't drop her, and I wasn't *going* to drop her."

"Uh-huh." Her expression told him she was unconvinced, and agreeing only to keep the peace. "Do you want some coffee?" Marta indicated the kitchen. "Sydney just made some."

Luc had tried to get some into him this morning, but Ike had left without it. His mind wasn't on his own needs. "No, I—"

"I think," she told him firmly, "you'd do better with some coffee."

He didn't feel like arguing. It wasn't worth it. His shoulders rose and fell apathetically. "Maybe—"

Marta had already begun to lead the way. As if sensing Ike wasn't following, she turned to look at him. She was right, he wasn't. "I'm sure you know your way into the kitchen better than I do."

"Yeah."

Ike made his way slowly into the next room. With the baby nestled against her, held fast with one arm, Marta already had a mug poured by the time he crossed the threshold.

"Black, right?" He raised his eyes questioningly at her. Her back to the stove, Marta held the mug out to him. "You had it that way last night." She answered his unspoken question. "I notice things about people."

And what Marta noticed about him now was that he was clearly shaken down to the core. Last night he'd told her that he didn't know where his sister was, now here he was this morning with her baby in his arms. What kind of crisis had taken place during the night while she'd been vainly trying to court sleep?

"Take it," she instructed sternly.

"Yes, ma'am." He took the mug in both hands. It bothered him that his hands shook a little. "Giving orders comes naturally to you."

"I've given my share." She studied his face. He'd had a worse night than she had, that was clear. "Would you like to talk about it?"

Ike stared into the dark mug, steeling himself from an onslaught of emotions he knew were waiting to ambush him. Sorrow, regret, anger—at himself and life. And guilt. They all came at once, assaulting him amid a ring of fire. If he gave way, they would all engulf him, burning him until there wasn't anything left. He couldn't afford that. He had Celine to care for.

"Nothing to talk about," he murmured. With supreme effort, he managed to keep his voice almost as light as it usually was.

He swallowed the hot brew, let it burn his tongue and his insides, wishing it could burn away the pain that was gnawing at his belly.

He'd left the house for Shayne's as soon as he thought it was civilized to do so, wanting to assure himself that the baby was all right. Last night, after he'd brought Celine upstairs, she'd cried for most of the night. He'd tried everything he could to quiet her, even as he tried to quiet all the emotions that were tumbling around inside him like clothes in a dryer gone haywire.

He'd succeeded at neither.

Luc had tried to help, sitting up part of the night with him. But there was no use in both of them losing sleep. Ike had sent him back to his room a little after one. He'd wanted to be alone anyway.

But he hadn't been alone. He'd had Celine. And his memories of his sister.

"What's going on, Ike?" Shayne walked into the room, concern etched across his unshaven face.

Ike instantly put down the mug. As he turned toward Shayne, he tried to shake off the dark mood encroaching on him. He struggled mightily for his easygoing smile, for the philosophical whimsy that had seen him through so much—the death of his own parents, Junie's abrupt disappearance and other, far more minor things.

The smile he flashed lacked conviction. "I brought you a brand-new patient." He passed a hand over the baby's head. She whimpered again. Feeling helpless, he dropped his hand again. "I figured things were slow for you."

Shayne lost no time crossing to the youngest member of Ike's family. Sydney had told him what she could. Disbelief still clung to him as he took the baby into his arms. But the black hair was a dead giveaway. The baby was a LeBlanc.

His eyes met Ike's. He could see how hard the man was struggling with his emotions. Ike and June had been very close once, Shayne remembered.

He smiled at Ike. "Thanks. You always did look out after my best interests."

A half smile curved Ike's mouth. "Talked Sydney into sticking it out, didn't I?"

"Yes, you did." Shayne indicated his small office in the back. "You want to come with me while I check her out?"

"No, I—" Ike paused. If he remained out here, he would be forced to stay with Sydney and Marta. He didn't think he could handle sympathy in any dosage at the moment. "Sure, maybe I'll learn something."

Walking out, Shayne stopped and began to sniff

the air. The smell hadn't been there a moment ago. "Sydney, is something—?"

The second Shayne began to ask the question, the smell penetrated and announced itself. Horrified, Marta whirled toward the stove. There were bright flames rising from the iron skillet. The oil was burning. The forgotten omelette was on its way to becoming charcoal. "Oh, my God!"

Closest to the stove, Ike came to life. With no time to think, he reacted, grabbing the lid from the counter and throwing it on top of the pan, smothering the flames. Grasping the hot skillet handle, he stifled a reflexive yelp as he deposited the pan into the sink. He'd almost dropped the pan on the wooden floor. Like a delayed reaction, pain shot from the palm of his hand up his arm through his shoulder until it stopped at the crown of his head.

Giving the baby to Marta, Shayne quickly crossed to Ike. "Let me see that."

Like a small boy caught doing something he shouldn't, Ike pulled his hand behind him. He hadn't come here to be fussed over. "It's nothing."

Nothing irritated Shayne more than a man trying to behave as if he were invulnerable. "Ike."

Ike blew out a breath. Reluctantly, he held his hand out and turned his palm upward for Shayne's perusal.

Shayne frowned. "'Nothing' is beginning to blister. Looks like I've got two patients." He looked toward his wife.

Intercepting the look, Marta read it correctly.

"Why don't I help you?" She smiled at the baby she was holding. "I'll hang onto the princess here while you tend to Asbestos Man." She indicated Ike with her eyes, and thought she saw a hint of a smile returning to his lips at the tease.

"I'll take all the help I can get." Shayne led the way into the small alcove that had, on more than one occasion, doubled as an emergency medical office. He glanced at his watch. It wasn't even eight o'clock yet. "Looks like this has the makings of a hell of a day."

As she walked out, Marta looked over her shoulder at Sydney. Dormant smoke hovered over the room like an ominous cloud. She felt guilty leaving Sydney to cope with it. "I'll help you clean up when I'm finished."

Sydney dismissed her with a quick wave. "You've got your hands full." She looked around the kitchen. Except for the burned skillet, it didn't look too bad. The exhaust fan over the stove would take care of most of the smoke and the smell of burned eggs. She switched it on and raised her voice. "Nothing here I can't handle."

Marta seriously doubted that there was anything in the world that Sydney couldn't handle. She walked into the small office in time to hear Ike protesting. "You don't have to fuss over my hand, Shayne. It's all right."

He opened the floor-to-ceiling medicine cabinet that had once served as a secondary pantry when his parents had lived here. Quickly, he gathered what he needed.

"Not yet, but it will be once I take care of it." Shayne placed the supplies he'd quickly gathered on a small table and beckoned Ike forward. He indicated where he wanted him to place his hand. "Otherwise, it's liable to get infected. Not much of a stretch from there to where gangrene sets in." He examined the wound more closely. If Ike had held the pan handle a couple of seconds longer, the wound would have turned into a really nasty one. "We're colorful enough around here without having a one-armed bartender in town."

Ike laughed. "You always did look on the bleak side of things."

"That way, happiness is a nice surprise." The way it was these days, Shayne added silently. He prepared the disinfectant. Casually, he asked, "Would you like to talk about it?"

Ike couldn't help glancing toward Marta. It was the second time in less than ten minutes that he'd had the exact same offer in the exact same words. Shrugging casually, he said, "You saw pretty much everything that was involved."

"About June."

Ike stoically stared straight ahead. "Don't have anything to say."

Very carefully, Shayne swabbed Ike's palm. Lucky for him, the burns were only first-degree. Ike didn't take inactivity well. And with Celine sud-

denly in his life, he wouldn't be able to remain
inactive even if he wanted to. "Where is she?"

Steeling himself off from both the sting in his
palm and the one in his heart, Ike replied, "Like
the song says, 'blowing in the wind.'"

Tossing aside one cotton swab, Shayne picked up
another. "Don't get metaphysical on me, Ike."

Ike watched the skin on his palm wither and
pucker as Shayne worked over it. If he kept his
mind on that, he could keep it off the words. "I'm
not."

How could he phrase the question now forming
in his mind? How did he ask his best friend something he knew hurt him even to say? But if nothing
else, as Celine's doctor he needed to know. He kept
his eyes on his work. "Is she dead?"

The small intake of breath drew Ike's attention
to Marta. He saw the sympathy in her eyes, and
blocked it. If he allowed himself to give in to it,
even for a moment, there was no telling what would
break loose inside him. He'd deal with all this later,
when he felt he was up to it.

"So the woman who brought me her baby says."

"You have any reason to doubt her?" The question came from Marta. Though she knew she had
no business asking, she couldn't get herself to just
stand on the sidelines, listening impassively.

Ike looked at her sharply, then allowed his look
to mellow. He shrugged carelessly, belying the tur-
moil within.

"No. She didn't ask me for money, or anything

else.'' He winced suddenly as Shayne applied a layer of something that stung like the devil. The disinfectant paled in comparison. Slowly, he let out a breath, realizing that a ring of perspiration had formed all along his hairline. ''If that's supposed to distract me, I'd just as soon have a pretty woman to look at, if you don't mind.'' He looked toward Marta.

This time, because he was hurting on more than one score, she didn't turn away.

''Won't be as good for your wound,'' Shayne quipped. ''But it certainly couldn't hurt.'' Working quickly, he began bandaging the injured hand. ''Who was this woman who brought Celine?''

Ike shook his head. ''I never saw her before. Said her name was Ruth Jackson. I found out she hired a pilot to fly her in here. She told me she worked with June at a makeup counter at some department store.'' He couldn't remember the name of the store, but it really didn't matter now. He continued struggling for control, for level ground. ''Did you know she only got as far as Fairbanks? All those great plans, and Junie only made it to Fairbanks. Might as well have stayed here.'' He pressed his lips together, trying not to think. Unable to do anything else. ''Should have stayed here.''

Shayne reached for the tape and was surprised when Marta handed it to him. ''Thanks.'' He turned his attention back to Ike. ''Do you know who the father is?''

''Yeah, that damn guitar player she ran off

with.'' At the very thought of the man, Ike's anger rose to a dangerous level. He struggled with that, too. No matter what he thought of Roy Watkins, the man was Celine's father. It put Ike at a distinct disadvantage. ''He left her. Didn't want to be saddled with Junie once he knew she was pregnant. Said he had no intention of looking after a 'brat.'''

Marta looked down at the baby in her arms. ''You're not a brat, are you sweetie?'' Celine was an orphan, just as she had been. Oh, Marta had had a mother, floating around somewhere, who'd wanted no part of her, and a nameless father who'd never come forward, but they might as well have been dead for all their input into her life. Just phantoms passing through, nothing more.

A bittersweet feeling filled her as she held the baby closer. Marta felt a bond form between her and the infant, a kinship.

Finishing up, Shayne surveyed his work. He spared Ike a glance. Another difficult topic to broach. Would Ike be relieved or angry to hear it? ''You know, the Langleys have been trying for a baby now for four years—''

''No.'' The word was uttered quietly, but firm for all that.

Was that love or guilt talking? Shayne wanted Ike to think this over carefully. ''Celine'd never want for anything—''

''No,'' Ike repeated more fiercely. ''I can give her anything she wants, anything she needs.'' There was a look of defiance in his eyes that Shayne had seldom seen. "I'm keeping her. I'm her family. She's Junie's daughter, and I'm keeping her. Junie signed a paper giving me sole, legal custody." He had it in his safe. Ruth had given him the document before she'd left, a piece of paper with his sister's faint signature on it, witnessed by the doctor who couldn't save her. It would hold up anywhere.

"How are you going to take care of her and run the saloon, too?"

He'd come here silently seeking support, not a devil's advocate. "I'll find a way." Ike tried to pull his thoughts together. "I've got Luc. We'll work something out."

Shayne looked down at the hand he'd just bandaged. "For starters, how are you going to manage with just one hand?"

Ike pulled it to his side. It throbbed and pulsed just as badly as when the initial burn had set in. He gritted his teeth. "I didn't break it. I burned it."

"Try handling something with that hand right now and see how it feels." Shayne knew that wouldn't even be necessary. Unless there was something about Ike's ability to heal that he was unaware of, the hand was hurting him even as they spoke.

"I can help."

Both men turned to look at Marta with unabashed surprise. Judging by their expressions, Ike's surprise was even greater than Shayne's.

She supposed that they weren't any more surprised by the offer than she was. But it wasn't in her nature to stand idly by when someone needed help, and there had to be some decency in Ike, since he was so willing to take in his sister's child. There was no law that he had to. Just as there was no law that said that a mother had to keep her child if she didn't want it, as long as she went through the proper channels to be rid of the obligation.

That put Ike at least one up on her own mother.

Marta shrugged, not wanting to make a big deal of her offer. "I'm here for a couple of weeks. I can divide my time between visiting with Sydney and taking care of Celine."

Ike had to admit, watching her, that she seemed to have an affinity for Celine. "Why would you do that?"

She looked at him. "Let's just say I have a weakness for babies. There's not very much you can do for her with your hand all bandaged up like that. You were at a disadvantage even before that." After a pause, she gave him his due and added, "And I also have a weakness for people who are willing to take on responsibilities."

She'd made it clear that she was determined not to like him. This was an about-face. "Is that the way to your heart?"

"Leave my heart out of this." She narrowed her eyes as she tried to regain ground. She didn't want him misunderstanding her motive. "Take it or leave it."

"I'll take it." He looked quizzically at Shayne as the latter placed a sling around his neck. "I never look a gift horse in the mouth. That goes double for a beautiful angel of mercy.''

Well, he had certainly bounced back quickly, Marta thought. Was she being too softhearted, volunteering to help him this way? Or was that soft-headed?

She wasn't helping him, she amended, she was helping this poor motherless baby. But at least Celine would never know the pain of discovering that her mother had sent her away willingly.

"What's this?" Ike tugged on the sling Shayne had just tied around his neck.

"It's a sling."

"I know it's a sling." Unaccustomed to being confined, he struggled to be patient. "What's it doing around my neck?"

"In place of a noose?" Marta suggested sweetly.

"It's to put your hand through." Gingerly, Shayne positioned it for him. "I want you to rest it for at least twenty-four hours. Your firefighting days are going to have to be put on hold for now." He glanced at Marta. "Looks like you came along just in time."

That, she thought, was a matter of opinion. But she'd volunteered and there was no backing out, not with a clear conscience.

"Doctor—" turning, she presented Celine to him "—I believe you have another patient to tend to now."

Shayne grinned. "Ever think of being a nurse? I could certainly use one."

"All I have is first-aid training."

"We all have to start somewhere," he murmured. Laying Celine down on the table, he began to slip off her shirt. "And with Sydney needing her rest, I could use the extra help."

A little overwhelmed, Marta could only shake her head and laugh. "You people certainly do make a woman feel wanted around here."

Ike smiled at her. All his other feelings were banked down for now, and he struggled for his identity. "Darlin', you don't know the half of it."

The look she saw in his eyes had her feeling just the slightest bit uncertain, and more than a little unsettled.

Chapter Seven

"You've decided to put her to work advertising the saloon?" Marta asked bemused. She was staring down at the red cloth affixed to Celine's bottom with the words "The Salty Saloon" written across the middle.

It wasn't often that Ike felt at a loss. He was a man who made his own way in the world, expecting nothing from anyone and being pleasantly surprised when he received something anyway. But Celine's appearance in his world had changed a few of his known parameters. He'd had to rely on invention and inspiration.

Ike spread the one hand he had at his disposal in a semi-surrender. "It's one of the napkins from the Salty. She was wet, I didn't have anything else to use.'' He looked at Shayne, who wasn't even trying to hold back his laughter. ''It's not as if I could send Luc out to the corner supermarket to get a fresh package of diapers in the middle of the night.''

Marta took charge of the napkin after Shayne took it off Celine. Thank God, Sydney had taken to stockpiling diapers. They were going to have to temporarily dip into her cache until Celine had her own supply.

About to fold up the wet napkin, Marta noticed a pasty whitish residue clinging to the inside. She looked at Ike suspiciously. ''What did you use for powder?''

''Cornstarch.'' It was a case of making do with what he had, and he'd vaguely remembered hearing that the product could be substituted for powder.

Cornstarch. She supposed it was a viable substitute, in a pinch—no pun intended, she silently amended, glancing toward Celine.

Tiny, thin legs were kicking up a storm, as if the infant was privy to some tune they couldn't hear and was marching to it.

''Lucky for Celine you didn't use flour and turn her into a popover.'' Unable to resist, Marta bent over and kissed one of the little feet. Her heart was lost on the next kick.

For the first time since he'd walked into the Salty and learned the reason for Ruth Jackson's appearance, Ike laughed. The laugh mellowed into a smile that graced his lips as he looked down at the baby on Shayne's makeshift examining table. It wasn't Celine's fault that Junie had died. Ike was already tucking the tiny being into his heart.

"She'd hardly make more than two bites. Maybe not even that."

There was affection in his voice. Affection in the look he bestowed on the baby. Whatever else Ike LeBlanc might be or have been, Marta thought, he did seem to have a heart.

At least, she qualified silently, he had one where a motherless infant was concerned. Giving him credit for anything more was being unnecessarily lenient, and possibly opening herself up for something she had no desire to cope with.

"Well, let's just see how many bites she would make." Having divested her of her clothing, Shayne picked Celine up and placed her on a scale. He recalibrated, making a minor adjustment for the weight of the blanket he'd placed across it.

Marta raised her eyes from the scale to Shayne. "A postage scale?"

Shayne laughed at the skepticism in Marta's voice, noticing that Ike, at least, seemed to take this in stride. But then, Ike was accustomed to improvising as much as he was. Here in Hades, more times than he liked to think about, it was the only way.

"It does the trick," Shayne assured her. "I have a real scale in my office." But that required twenty-five minutes of travel, and he had a feeling that Ike wanted to get this over with as soon as possible.

Heading a piece of paper with Celine's name on it, Shayne jotted down her weight. "Out here, you learn to make do."

"Obviously." She supposed there was something to be said for that, for having your initiative prodded and stirred. But it was the monotony counterbalanced with the life-and-death situations that would have gotten to her, were she forced to live in a place like this.

Ike looked at Marta sharply. The tone of her voice was almost identical to the one Junie had used. Time had done nothing to mute the dissatisfaction he'd heard in her voice back then. The dissatisfaction and the yearning.

And now that voice was forever stilled.

He pushed the memory as far away as he was able. It wouldn't do anyone any good to dwell on that now. Celine needed him. He had to stay focused on that and not allow himself to be sidetracked. By anything.

Sydney looked up as Shayne and the others walked out of the study. "Well?"

"I'm happy to say that Hades's newest citizen is healthy and thriving." A look that was only slightly dubious came into his eyes as he directed them toward Ike. "Think you can keep her that way?"

"With a little help from my friends," Ike allowed, looking significantly at Marta.

She was hardly his friend, Marta thought, just someone who'd been enlisted. No, that wasn't strictly true. This was of her own making. No one had twisted her arm.

Marta saw the puzzled expression on Sydney's face. "I volunteered to help him get his feet wet."

Sydney zeroed in what Marta had just said. Well, well, well. It looked as if things might be moving along in an orderly fashion after all. The trick with Marta, Sydney recalled now, was not to push, just to position her to be in the right place at the right time.

Sydney smiled, looking pleased. "You can always count on Marta to come through when you need her."

"Well, I need her," Ike agreed wholeheartedly. "There's no doubt about that."

Maybe she was being unduly suspicious, but Marta could have sworn there was something in his tone that went beyond just needing someone to help him out for a few days. If he meant to take advantage of this opportunity, he was going to be disappointed. The only one she intended to care for was Celine.

Drawn by the commotion going on in the living room, Sara and Mac came bounding down the stairs, still dressed in their pajamas. They sounded like an army instead of just two children, neither of whom weighed an ounce more than seventy pounds.

Sleep instantly vanished from Sara's eyes as they widened, staring at the baby in Marta's arms. Her mouth dropped open.

"Mommy, you had the baby," Sara accused. She flew over to Marta, then stood on her toes for a better view. Her small mouth closed into a petulant pout. "You weren't supposed to do that without telling me."

Three years older and desperate to be worldly, Mac frowned at his sister's obvious naiveté.

"She didn't have the baby, stupid. She's still fat." The words were no sooner out of his mouth than Mac flushed. Even at his tender age, he realized he'd just committed a horrible social error. He looked at Sydney, tongue-tied, oblivious to the fact that his father was laughing. "I didn't mean—"

Nodding, Sydney slipped an arm around his slim shoulders. "That's all right, Mac, I *am* fat."

Shayne brushed a kiss on his wife's temple as he laid a hand on her swollen belly. "But only in the very nicest sense of the word," he qualified for his son.

Ike pretended to ward off a shiver that went down his spine. "Lucky thing I took my coffee black. There's enough sugar floating around here to rival the final harvest at a sugarcane plantation."

Her attention still focused on the baby, Sara stared at Ike, clearly lost. She shifted her eyes toward Marta and the baby in her arms. "Whose baby *is* it?" she asked impatiently.

"It's Ike's," Shayne told her.

"No," Sara said, looking confused. "Men can't have babies."

"Not by themselves," Ike agreed, looking at Marta. "But Marta's helping me."

"You mean the baby's yours and Marta's?" Mac's mouth fell open. His dad had told him all about this mysterious process of creating people. He couldn't say he much cared for it, but his dad had said it was true, so it had to be. Dubious now of the information he'd just been given, his eyes swept over Marta's flat stomach. "When did you get— you know—?"

Trying not to laugh at the befuddled expression on his very serious son's face, Shayne untangled the knot for him. "The baby is Ike's niece, and we're all going to help him take care of her."

Mac zeroed in on the only thing of importance that had been conveyed. "Oh, it's a girl." The frown on his young face deepened twofold.

In a gesture of camaraderie, Ike confided, "Someday, boy, if you're going to live around here, you're not going to say 'girl' in exactly that tone of voice." He winked when Mac looked up at him quizzically. "You'll cheer, I guarantee it."

"Uh-huh," Mac said, turning toward the breakfast his mother had prepared.

But if Mac's interest had faded, Sara's had only sharpened. She raised her eyes to Marta. "What's her name?" she asked.

"Celine," Ike answered.

Sara acknowledged him with a quick turn of her head. But though her heart belonged to Ike, it was obvious that she thought Marta was in charge here. "Can I hold her?" she asked hopefully.

Ike looked dubious, but Marta had already taken Sara's hand in hers and was leading the little girl over to the leather sofa. "Why don't you get up there and sit down?"

Sara was quick to do what she was told. Seated, she stretched out her arms expectantly, holding her breath.

Very carefully, Marta placed the baby into Sara's arms. "Keep her head up, like so," Marta instructed, positioning Sara. "And Sara?"

"Yes?"

"It's okay to breathe," she whispered.

Sara beamed and exhaled the breath she'd been holding. Her eyes widened again as she saw Celine looking up at her with what could have passed for a smile on her small lips. Sara certainly took it to be one. "She likes me."

"That's 'cause she's little and don't know no better," Mac called out from the kitchen, his mouth stuffed with waffle.

"Don't pay any attention to him," Marta told her. "You're doing fine." She glanced over at Mac. He was trying to appear nonchalant, but it was clear to Marta that he was trying a little too hard. "You'll have your turn," she promised. He lowered his head, inordinately preoccupied with his waffle. "And you—" Marta looked at Ike, surprising him "—could stand to learn a little something from Sara here. Even she holds the baby better than you do."

Ike nodded his head in acknowledgment. "Must be a female thing."

Marta crossed her arms before her, fixing him with an unimpressed look. "Good excuse. Doesn't wash."

Ike glanced at Sydney. "Takes right over, doesn't she?" He didn't bother waiting for her to comment. "She's probably trying to compensate for the fact that she's short."

"I'm not short. I'm petite," Marta countered, her chin slightly raised. She watched Sara for a moment longer. The little girl was enjoying herself; she took to mothering naturally.

Backing away, she whispered to Sydney, "Looks like you're going to be getting a lot of good help when the time comes."

Hearing her, Sara looked up and beamed at the compliment.

She was good with kids, Ike thought, looking at Marta. It wasn't a quality he would ever have thought he'd find immensely comforting.

But he did.

The smell of wood was evident even before she closed the door behind her. It pervaded almost everything within the small general store, fusing itself with the air until it was all one and the same. She wondered if the smell had gotten to the tall, wide pock-faced man behind the counter. Sporting an apron that might have been white a quarter of a century ago but was now a very dull, worn gray,

Tate Kellogg gave the impression of being asleep on his feet. She'd thought he was a statue when she'd first walked in, until Ike had greeted him. Kellogg had grunted something in return.

Whether it had been an actual word or just indigestion was anyone's guess, Marta thought. He'd grimaced a half smile when he'd noticed her. She'd nodded in return.

"That's Tate Kellogg. He doesn't like to waste words," Ike told her under his breath.

"I guess he's saving them for something important." No doubt about it. Living here would drive her crazy in a week. Maybe less.

"You never know," Ike countered, following her.

Closer than a shadow, his breath slid along the back of her neck, making her shiver. She hoped he hadn't noticed. Looking up, she saw his reflection in the windowpane and knew her hope was futile. Ike was smiling to himself.

Walking along the short, narrow aisles, looking at the paltry selection of items was a culture shock for Marta, to say the least. Accustomed to a mad profusion of goods, of being faced with a wide variety of choices for every item she wanted, the shelves of Kellogg's General Store were a disappointment.

The small section reserved for Baby Items was woefully understocked. She picked up a box of dry formula, then put it back. It wasn't what she wanted. She thought of the pantry at Shayne's. Sydney must have cleared out the store's supply, even though there hadn't been all that much. "Don't you people have babies out here?"

There was something almost stirring about the woman when she was trying to suppress her annoyance, he thought. "Well, I can't speak for everyone, but I didn't until last night."

The soft, indolent smile that she'd noticed yesterday at the airport had made a comeback. Looking at him, Marta decided that he'd gotten over his grief rather quickly. Obviously, the man healed fast, but that wasn't any of her business one way or another. She'd volunteered to help, mainly because she felt the baby deserved a fighting chance to survive within this new set of circumstances. Roving bachelors usually didn't have many child-rearing skills.

And she'd volunteered because he'd gotten to her, she had to admit. Gotten to her by being so adamant about keeping his word to a woman who could no longer take him to task for breaking it.

That had to mean something in the scheme of things.

Sydney had offered to give Ike some of her things, but he'd demurred, saying he could get what he needed from the general store. Obviously the man was possessed of an optimistic streak that was completely baseless.

If he was serious about raising Celine, he was going to need a myriad of things: clothes, food, furnishings. Frustrated, she turned from the pitiful selection. "Where did Sydney get her things?"

"Anchorage." He'd even accompanied her on several trips to help her carry the various purchases when Shayne was busy at the clinic.

Anchorage. Reachable only by plane. Her stomach lurched and knotted at the very thought. But the problem went beyond her own reluctance to fly. They needed a pilot. "And she and Shayne are the only pilots?"

He should never have put off the lessons, he thought. Ike nodded, following her down the next aisle. "Except when Kellogg's son Jeb comes to visit. But that's not very often these days."

Marta stopped abruptly. The next aisle had a minuscule selection of pails, mops and cleaning products. No more baby products. The store could definitely stand an overhaul.

"Small wonder," she murmured. Given a choice, she wouldn't voluntarily come out here, either. "Well, if you're going to be a functioning uncle, we need to get to Anchorage." She looked down at the only items she'd chosen: the last two packages of disposable diapers. Only one was infant-size. The second was the next size up. That meant they were going to be using a lot of extra tape. "There's not enough here to keep her in diapers through the week."

Her offhand remark was jarring. He looked down at the two large packages. Together, that added up to a lot of diapers. "They go through that many?"

The naive question made her smile. Walking up to the counter, she placed both packages down and stepped back so that he could pay. "You really don't know anything about babies, do you?"

He tried to reach for his wallet, only to realize that it was on the wrong side. He looked at Marta with an unspoken request. With a sigh, she reached into his pocket for him. He smiled as her hand slid in and extracted the wallet.

"Only that half of them grow up to be beautiful women. You've got a light touch."

"It can be heavy when it has to be." Marta dropped the wallet on the counter. "As for the charm, save it for somebody who can appreciate it." Her voice was clipped, impersonal. "I'm only here to help."

Fishing out several bills, he handed them to the storekeeper. Kellogg appeared to be stoically oblivious to the conversation that was going on. "And you can't appreciate a compliment?"

Marta's eyes met his, purposely ignoring the warm sensation they generated as they returned her gaze. "I appreciate sincerity."

Ike saw no conflict. "Compliments can be sincere." He accepted the change Kellogg gave him, pocketed it along with the wallet, then picked up the first package.

Rather than watch him struggle trying to juggle the two, Marta picked up the second package and led the way out of the store. "Not if the compliments are coming from a man who can spout them like a spigot that's been left turned on." His car was parked right outside the store. She waited as he opened the trunk, then tossed the diapers in. "You're going to have to make a run to Anchorage. There's no way around it."

He slammed the trunk shut. "Is that an editorial 'you'?"

Because of his injured hand, he'd had her drive to the store. She waited as he unlocked the door on the driver's side. "Meaning?"

He rounded the hood to the passenger side and got in. "That you're going to come with me, right?"

Sliding in behind the wheel, she buckled up, avoiding looking at his face. But somehow she could still tell that Ike was smiling. And that smile somehow managed to seep into her being.

"You don't need me to hold your hand."

"That's a matter of opinion. Um, would you mind?" He looked down at the seat belt.

With a sigh, she reached over and pulled the belt around him, a little too aware of how close her hand brushed as she brought the belt around to the slot.

"Thanks. As for Anchorage, I'd like you to show me what I need."

Hands on the wheel, she looked at him. "You're that helpless?"

The expression on his face was pure innocence. Or as innocent as someone like Ike could be. "Yes."

Of course she could say no. After all, it was just a ploy. But then she thought of the tiny baby they'd left with Sydney. She sighed. Turning the key, she started up the engine.

"I guess there's something to be said for a man who's honest enough to admit his shortcomings."

Ike leaned back, satisfied he'd accomplished what he set out to do. "Darlin', someday you'll learn that I am always honest."

She glanced in her rearview mirror, then almost laughed at herself for doing it. Traffic here meant another car somewhere in the same general vicinity. She pulled away from the curb. "There aren't enough somedays in an eternity for that to happen."

It was on the tip of her tongue to turn him down, to tell Ike that she could give him a list to take with him. But she knew that wouldn't be enough. Things would occur to her once she was in the baby department. Things that probably wouldn't occur to him if he went by himself. Or even with Shayne. She didn't like the idea of having to fly again so soon after her last experience, but there didn't seem to be a way around it. Not if her conscience was to remain clear.

He could see the mental battle going on and decided to tip the scales. "For Celine?"

"*Only* for Celine," Marta underscored, then capitulated. "All right, let's go ask Shayne if he's free for a couple of hours."

With his one free arm, he embraced her, surprising Marta. "On behalf of Celine, I thank you."

The kiss he brushed against her cheek came as a complete shock. Not because he kissed her—that she would have expected—but because he'd kissed her cheek instead of her lips. They were stopped at one of the three lights in town. And even if they hadn't been, there was precious little chance of her hitting man, beast or car even if she were driving. She would have expected Ike to take full advantage of the situation. That he didn't left her confused and bewildered. Unable to affix a proper label to him, she pushed the incident aside, choosing not to think about it. She wasn't in the mood for riddles.

Instead, she hid behind a resigned sigh. "Might as well get this over with as soon as possible."

"Not quite that soon," he told her. The smile faded just a little. "There's someplace I have to go first."

There was something in his tone that made her look at him sharply. "Where?"

Ike thought of being evasive, then saw no point. "Fairbanks." He'd already spoken to Shayne about it. He wanted to see where Junie had lived these last few months. He owed it to her.

Marta felt her heart wrench at the look in his eyes. She heard herself saying, "I'm coming with you," and had no idea why, except perhaps that she never liked seeing anyone in pain. And it was suddenly apparent to her that he still was. She hadn't a clue what to do about it, but knew she had to be there with him.

Chapter Eight

The small, one-room apartment in Fairbanks was almost stark. Its orientation barred the attendance of any sunlight, casting a pall within its confines. It was as if it, too, was in mourning, Ike thought, looking around slowly.

This was where Junie had lived, where she had made plans for her baby and kept herself hidden from him.

Almost in a trance, Ike moved about the apartment, trying to feel his sister, to get a sense of something that had resided here other than despair. If there had been something else, it eluded him.

The landlord who had allowed him this last glimpse into Junie's world was standing out in the hall, waiting. Shayne had used the pretext of looking up an old friend from medical school to allow him this time alone. Only Marta had stubbornly insisted on coming inside. She stood off to the side now, silent for once.

"I should have done more," he said to himself under his breath.

Marta had thought that herself when he'd first mentioned his sister, had accused him of not caring and lumped him together with all the people who hadn't cared in her own life. But looking at him now told her she'd been wrong. He did care—a great deal. And he was torturing himself.

"And done what?" she asked softly.

Ike turned around, surprised by the sound of her voice. He'd forgotten for a moment that she was here, too, having planted herself in his wake. She was standing in the shadows that the room embraced so eagerly. He shrugged, helpless and fighting not to be overwhelmed. "Something. Brought her back."

"Dragging her by her hair?" He looked at her sharply. Marta approached him slowly, the way she would have a wounded animal. Because he *was* wounded. "She made her choice," she pointed out gently.

"She was *eighteen* when she left." The self-accusation throbbed in his voice. "At eighteen, you don't understand the choices."

"But you struggle to try. That's how you learn. You couldn't live her life for her."

Ike fought to keep the tears back. They wouldn't

do Junie any good now. He dismissed Marta's words. "I could have protected her."

Moving solely on instinct, she laid her hand on his arm. "She didn't want your protection. And it wouldn't have counted unless she tried to protect herself." She'd learned that herself, the hard way.

Ike waved her words away with a vague hand. And then he saw the lone framed photograph standing forlornly on the table—a broken-down kitchen table whose only company was a mismatched pair of chairs on either side. His throat closed as he reached for it. The photograph was of the two of them, taken the day he'd graduated from high school. Junie was laughing. He remembered saying something to tease her just before the photograph was taken. It was his favorite one of the two of them.

Standing beside him, Marta looked down at it. "She was very beautiful."

"Yes," he said quietly, "she was."

There was little else in the apartment. A handful of clothes hanging in the closet, clothes he recognized. Junie hadn't even bought herself anything new in the three years she'd been gone. Beyond that, there was nothing, no knickknacks, no signs of the bright young woman she'd been on her way to becoming. She'd traded all that for the promise of things that never came to be.

If he had Roy in front of him right now—Celine's father or not—he would kill him, Ike thought.

The landlord, a heavyset, bald man, poked his head in. "You about through in here?"

Ike picked up the photograph again. "Yeah, we're through." He walked past the other man.

Slightly befuddled, the landlord looked after him. "What do you want me to do with her things?"

Ike didn't even pause. His fingers tightened around the frame. "Give them to charity. I have all that I want."

With a shake of his head, Shayne looked at all the purchases Ike and Marta were unloading from the taxi they'd used to get to Fairbanks Airport's airfield. It was several hours later. After Ike had left Junie's apartment, Marta had insisted they go straight to the department stores and shop for Celine. He had a hunch she thought of it as therapy. Shayne hoped that there was enough room in the cargo hold.

"And I thought Sydney was bad when she came home from her last shopping spree." He began loading the bags while Ike paid the driver. "You look like you cleared out half the stores in Fairbanks."

"Just the essentials," Marta replied.

"Any more 'essentials,'" Shayne commented, contemplating the infant seat Marta had just taken out of the taxi's trunk, "and we might have had to hire a cargo plane to make the flight back to Hades with us."

Pocketing his change, Ike went to help finish unloading the trunk. He was silently grateful that Marta had taken charge the way she had, allowing him no time to think about what he'd just seen. It was all he could do just to keep up with her. He grinned to himself. The woman had been like a heat-seeking missile, maneuvering from one counter to another, one store to the next.

"Already done. There's furniture flying in in a couple of days." Ike shook his head. "There's no holding the lady back once she gets started."

He glanced in Marta's direction. Ike couldn't help wondering if the same thing was true in all other facets in her life. Was she this enthusiastic, this unbridled when she made love with a man? When she finally let her reserve drop away and gave herself freely? It was something he knew he would really enjoy discovering firsthand.

"Move out of the way," Marta told Ike, elbowing him aside, away from the cargo hold. "I can do this faster with my own two hands."

Ike grinned, stepping back. At least she wasn't the type who expected to be waited on hand and foot. He rather liked her independent nature. It was a pleasant change from a lot of women he knew. It just needed a little fine tuning. "Really like having your way with things, don't you?"

She wasn't sure what he was implying. "Like has nothing to do with it. It's just more efficient my way, that's all."

"Uh-huh." Ike exchanged looks with Shayne over Marta's head. The latter looked amused, turning away when Marta glanced in his direction. Using his one good hand, Ike picked up one of the sacks containing the formula that Shayne had recommended. "Whatever you say."

"So, how's my girl?" Ike asked, walking into the house. Determined to put everything he'd seen in the small apartment in Fairbanks behind him, Ike looked around for Celine. His free arm laced with shopping bag loops, he made his way into the living room before depositing them on the sofa. Bags sagged against one another, sighing and spilling their contents.

"I'm fine," Sara piped up. "So's Celine. I took good care of her, didn't I, Mommy?"

"The best," Sydney agreed. With effort, she raised herself up from her seat.

"And I appreciate that." Ike produced a toy, handing it to the little girl. "And I brought you something to thank you."

Surprised, Marta wondered when he had had a chance to purchase the small stuffed cat. To her recollection, they had done all the shopping together. Ike's eyes met hers and he smiled, as if reading her thoughts.

"Ooh, thank you." Sara hugged the toy to her. "I'll call it Ike."

"Better not," he cautioned. He tugged on the pink pants the cat was wearing. "It's a girl."

"Oh." Sara giggled over her mistake. "Just like

Taffy,'' she said, referring to the cat Sydney had given her the first Christmas they had shared.

''And how's my other girl?'' he asked, turning toward Sydney.

''If you mean Celine, she's asleep. I just put her down ten minutes ago.''

''She's using the baby's new crib,'' Sara told him importantly.

''Breaking it in, is she?'' Sara nodded vigorously. ''Let's go see her.''

Marta watched him take Sara's hand and hurry up the stairs with the little girl. She had to admit, his eagerness surprised her.

''He's going to make a good father,'' Sydney said to Shayne.

Shayne nodded. ''I never pictured him in that role, but I think you're right. Good thing for Celine. Wait until you see the furniture he's having shipped for her.''

''I just hope they don't—'' Sydney didn't get a chance to finish her sentence. The baby was crying. ''They did.'' She looked reluctantly at the stairs. ''Well, he's not going to be able to pick her up out of the crib with that hand. And I don't think Sara should try—''

Shayne put his hand on her arm, stopping her. ''Stay. I'll go up.''

''You both stay,'' Marta instructed. She took the stairs two at a time.

''I used to have energy like that,'' she heard Sydney say wistfully.

"Don't worry," Shayne told her. "It'll all come back to you." He saw the questioning look in his wife's eyes and understood. He nodded. "He's going to be all right."

Sydney let out a sigh of relief.

Witnessing the silent communication between them, a feeling of envy wafted over Marta again even though she tried to bank it down. Envy at what Sydney had and what she was certain she would never have. Love, a home, a family. She'd thought she was on the verge once with Alex, but that had turned into a disaster. She wasn't willing to risk her heart again, even for a prize as grand as what Sydney had. Sydney was lucky. But good men were hard to find and Marta didn't feel particularly lucky. She'd never been, there was no reason to start believing that anything had changed now.

When she came into the room, she saw that Ike had taken his sling from around his arm and was attempting to pick Celine up.

"Wait," Marta ordered, crossing to him. "One of you is bound to get hurt." Carefully, she took the baby from the crib.

Ike smiled. "Thanks for looking out for me."

"I was thinking more of Celine." She nodded at his arm. "Ready?"

"Always."

Because Sara was in the room, she didn't say what immediately came to mind. Instead, she just placed Celine in his arms. The baby quieted down immediately. "A few days old and she's spoiled already."

"They don't spoil at this age," he countered, looking down at the tiny face that had already won his heart. "They're too fresh."

"You're getting better at it," Marta observed.

"It just takes practice." He glanced at her. "Some things come naturally to me, other things I have to work at."

She wished he wouldn't look at her like that. With everything she'd been through, it wasn't supposed to affect her. But that was logic speaking, and it wasn't logic that was being affected.

"I think she just wants some company. What do you think, darlin'?" His question was directed to Sara, who looked very pleased at being included in the adult conversation.

"I think you're right. Little kids don't like being left alone."

He looked at Marta. "I like consulting with experts whenever possible." Then he grinned at Sara. "Then I guess we'll just have to take her downstairs, won't we?" Sara's head bobbed up and down.

"Back again?" Sydney asked when they came downstairs. She was looking at the baby as she said it.

"She wants company," Sara declared.

"How would you know?" Mac challenged. He was sitting on the sofa, schoolbooks spread out in all directions.

"'Cause I'm an expert. Ike says so," she added when her brother hooted.

"That's enough, kids," Shayne said sternly, walking in with the last of the bags.

"Oh, Shayne, I'm sorry, I should have helped." Guilt nipped at Marta for having left Shayne to bring in all the packages.

Shayne shook his head. "No problem. These days, I don't get as much exercise as I should." He smiled significantly at his wife.

"Show me everything," Sydney entreated, her eyes sweeping along the cache of goods on the floor.

Laid out this way, it certainly looked like quite a haul, Ike thought. He laughed, turning toward Sydney. "You have no idea what you're in for. Your friend shops as if they were about to declare possession of money a major felony and she only had until dawn to get rid of a huge quantity." He grinned easily, glancing at Marta. "Pretty good at spending other people's money, aren't you?"

He saw the strange look that entered Marta's eyes, saw her closing off. "What?"

Marta shook her head. "Nothing." Abruptly, she crossed to the front door. "Excuse me for a minute," she murmured to Sydney just before she went out.

Confused, Ike handed Celine to Sydney and quickly followed Marta out the door. He found her standing a few yards away, staring off at the horizon.

"If I said something to offend you, darlin', I'm sorry."

She didn't bother turning around. She might have known he couldn't leave her alone. "I said it was nothing."

Her voice was almost as cold as the weather, but he wasn't about to let it put him off. Since she wasn't turning around, he circled Marta until he was in front of her. "Your mouth did. Your eyes said something else. I'm very good at reading eyes."

"Oh?" Her eyes narrowed as she regarded him. "Then what are mine saying right now?"

He laughed. "I don't think that's anatomically possible."

"Very good," she conceded with a laugh despite herself. "Maybe you can read eyes at that."

That look was still there. She was trying to distract him, but it was still there—the look that said he'd somehow hurt her. "Was it the crack about spending other people's money? I didn't mean anything by it."

She shrugged, rubbing her hands along her arms. Even still wearing her parka, she felt cold. Why would anyone in their right mind ever make the choice to stay when they could leave?

"I know. Sometimes I overreact."

She didn't believe that, he thought. "You're still not answering me."

She turned, an enigmatic expression crossing her lips. There was no way she was about to tell him that someone had accused her of that very thing when she was fifteen. The foster father she'd had at the time had discovered that she'd spent three dollars more than she'd been instructed to. He'd sent her to the supermarket on an errand and had become enraged when she hadn't returned with the proper change. When he'd discovered the item he'd wanted had gone up in price, he'd made a half-hearted stab at apologizing, but the scar was already there.

"I know." With that, she walked back inside. If she was going to be in what amounted to two places at once, she had her work cut out for her. Timing was everything.

"Are you sure you don't mind my leaving?" Marta looked at Sydney, wavering.

She knew she'd volunteered, but now that she was about to go with Ike, she had her doubts about the wisdom of her offer. Marta glanced toward Ike. A lot of doubts. Not the least of which was that she didn't like the idea of leaving Sydney. After all, Sydney was the reason she'd come out here in the first place, not Ike.

Definitely not Ike, she silently underscored with feeling.

Sydney gave her a quick hug, correctly reading her concern. "Will you stop worrying? Go with him," she urged. "Ike needs you more than I do."

Though Marta hated to admit it, it was true. She'd only be keeping Sydney company. She'd be helping Ike. And Celine. It was Celine she focused on.

"All right, I'll go with Ike." Since she was going in Ike's car, there might be a problem about getting back. He wasn't to drive for the remainder of the day, and he did need his vehicle back. "Would it be too much trouble for Shayne to pick me up on his way home?"

"I can run you back," Ike said. "I don't need two hands."

Marta looked at him. "What about Celine?"

"She won't be driving for a few years, yet, will you, darlin'?"

Celine cooed in response, as if she were actually listening to him. How *did* he get females to do that? Marta wondered. "I mean, won't you have to stay with Celine?"

"Luc can watch her for me. Or we can put her in the back seat. We did buy that car seat for her."

The details could be worked out later, Marta thought. But in order to come back, she first had to leave. "All right, let's go." She kissed Sydney, then looked down at the stomach that got in the way. She placed a hand fondly on the swell. "You be good in there," she admonished.

Marta walked out with Ike, Celine in her arms. Ambivalent emotions ricocheted through her like kernels of popcorn exploding in a microwave. She hoped she wasn't making a huge mistake by agreeing to go back with him. She might feel as if she saw right through him, but there was something dangerously hypnotic about the way he looked at a woman.

As she'd observed, even Celine wasn't impervious.

Chapter Nine

"I think you should know that the men around here generally outnumber the women about five to one."

Bringing Ike's vehicle to a stop in the small garage he'd pointed out to her, Marta pulled up the hand brake and turned to look at him. Behind them, secure in her infant seat, Celine woke up as the car stopped moving. Tiny fussing noises began.

"Is there any particular reason you chose now to give me this little tidbit of touristy information?"

"I just wanted you to be prepared." He said it innocently enough. Doubting he'd ever known an innocent day in his life, Marta was wary.

She glanced toward the large, two-story building. The first floor was completely devoted to the Salty

Saloon. It looked too innocuous to be a den of in-
iquity, but then, hell probably didn't come with
neon signs either.

"And just what am I supposed to be prepared
for?" she asked suspiciously.

"To be stared at." He winked at her, reaching
over to release his seat belt. "More than usual.
Would you mind?" He indicated the release, unable
to quite get it himself.

Without glancing at it, she pressed the button and
the metal tongue slid out of its retainer. She was
too busy trying to ignore the effect of his wink.
Why would a simple movement of molecules and
atoms, cells and tissue, have almost the same effect
on her as being in a plane and dipping into an air
pocket? It was utterly absurd. Ike was just flirting
with her. The man flirted with every breath he took,
every step he made. She knew that. So why did that
wink get such a rise out of her? Or find her so
unprepared?

She *wasn't* unprepared, or at least she shouldn't
be. She'd walked this route before, knew there was
nothing but emptiness at the end. Having lived
through it all once should have bred a certain immunity in her.

The theory was sound, the execution of it, however, was far more shaky.

Getting out, she opened the rear passenger door
and unbuckled Celine before Ike could start fumbling with the belts. She wondered how much of
that was real and how much was strictly for her

benefit. He struck her as far too able a man to be impeded by a bandaged hand, even if his fingers were temporarily covered.

"I'd think," she murmured, protecting Celine's head as she drew the child from her seat, "that Celine would arouse more curiosity than I would."

Ordinarily, Ike might be inclined to agree with her. But Celine was a mere baby, while Marta was a full-fledged woman in every sense of the word. Had she been the hag from *Hansel and Gretel,* she would have attracted some male attention in Hades. Being so much more than that guaranteed her a captivated audience.

He tugged Celine's cap beneath her hood back into place just as Marta began picking her up.

"Word spreads fast around here, for all the distance between us. I'm sure they all already know about Celine." And about Junie, he added silently. A look, a nod, would generally convey one man's sympathies to another. There was no need for words. There was, in fact, a certain discomfort in voicing them. "Men like to avoid certain subjects."

She looked at him knowingly. "Like commitment."

"Like condolences," he corrected. "Out here, no matter what you might think, most men have an easier time committing than in the lower forty-nine."

She waited while he looked through the trunk, trying to locate the bag with Celine's formula. "Gives them somebody warm in bed?"

He glanced over his shoulder at her. Whoever had had this woman's heart before had really put it through the threshing machine, he decided. "Something like that."

Marta began to rock the infant, trying to divert Celine's attention as the baby's fussing increased in volume. She stared at Ike's back. The man was broader than Shayne, she thought, and his hair was a tad darker. That would be the Native American in him.

Why was she scrutinizing him? It didn't matter what he looked like or where his features came from.

"So why haven't you committed?" She knew the answer to that. For men like Ike, commitment was against their credo. But she was curious to hear what sort of a spin he'd put on it.

"Aha." Finding the bag he was looking for, Ike extracted it from the rest. Pleased, he turned around to look at Marta. The woman spent far too much time looking solemn, he thought. "Never quite found the right woman." His eyes smiled at her. "And I don't believe in settling."

There were no promises in his eyes, only a sheer appreciation of what he saw. Marta felt flattered. Beautiful.

And foolish if she bought into it, she told herself. She moved the top blanket so that it lightly covered Celine's face. It was time they fed the baby. "Okay, I've been forewarned. Let's go."

There was a moment, just after she followed Ike

inside and before the room fell silent, when she felt as if she'd stepped onto the set of a western.

Had she every word in the world at her disposal, she wouldn't have been able to find one that suited the surroundings better than *saloon*. From the crystal chandelier that refracted and played with a myriad of lights, making rainbows out of them, to its wooden walls, its darkly tinted mirror that ran the length of the actual bar, and the wide, colorful mural on the back wall, it was a saloon through and through.

There were perhaps forty-five men in total, either at the bar or seated at some of the freestanding tables or booths that were scattered around the premises. Ike hadn't exaggerated, Marta thought.

Judging by the polite and appreciative looks the men gave her, Marta knew a woman could easily have her head turned in a place like this if she wasn't careful. But she was nothing if not careful. She'd learned at least that much.

Marta squared her shoulders just a little as she met, without flinching, the unabashed scrutiny.

The man closest to the end of the bar shouted a greeting to Ike. "Hey, who's the new talent?" The grin was even wider than the man's grizzled, unshaven face.

"She's a lady, not 'talent,'" Ike informed the man easily. Was it her imagination, or had he taken a step closer to her as he said it? Was that his way of being protective, or just his method of staking a would-be claim? She warned herself against feeling safe, but something about his manner made it hard not to. "And I'd mind my manners if I were you."

Someone in the back laughed, pointing. "Looks like you didn't."

"What happened to your hand?" another man yelled out, his words sounding just the slightest bit slurred. Marta hugged the baby a little closer to her. When she felt Ike's hand on her shoulder, it took everything she had not to jump. Her nerves were closer to the surface than she'd thought.

He inclined his head close to her ear. "We're going through a slow stretch right now," Ike confided. "The men are kind of starved for excitement around here." His good hand still on her shoulder, he held up his bandaged hand for the others. "Let this be a lesson to all of you. The lady's too hot to handle."

A mixture of guffaws and comments—some, she realized, in French—met his announcement. Marta could feel color creeping up her cheeks and was grateful that the lighting in the Salty, despite the chandelier, wasn't the brightest. Annoyed at the comment and her own reaction to it, she shrugged his hand off, only to have her action met with more laughter.

"Well, if she's too hot for you, so much for me taking a shot," an older man bemoaned. He looked far more interested in the contents of his mug than in female companionship. He signaled to the man behind the bar. "Hey Jean Luc, bring another one over here."

"They don't mean anything by it," Ike assured her. He slipped his hand beneath her elbow, trying to usher her through the room. As they went, he nodded a greeting at several of the men. "They're a harmless bunch on the whole."

"On the whole," she echoed. "Comforting." Although, if asked, she'd have to say she'd seen worse leers on the faces of the men in a singles sports bar, the one and only time she'd been talked into going to one.

"It was meant to be." Still steering her toward the rear of the establishment, where the stairs leading to the living quarters were located, he nodded at the tall, muscular blond man behind the counter. "This is my cousin, Jean Luc."

For all the noise and apparent excitement, Jean Luc, she noticed, looked to be rather shy. She found herself taking an instant liking to him. "I sort of surmised that when that man bellowed his name. Hello, Jean Luc."

Ike laughed. "Nothing gets past you, does it? Luc, this is Marta, Sydney's friend, the one I was telling you about. She's going to give me a few pointers on taking care of the baby."

"Pointers on making a baby?" someone behind him called out, laughing. "You do not need any pointers, Ike. Or are you slipping?"

Turning, Ike saw that the comment had come from Yuri Ivanov. A mining foreman whose career had begun somewhere on the plains of Siberia, Yuri had come with the purchase of the bar. He'd been taking over that very same booth he was sitting in for as long as anyone could remember. Every large family had a crazy uncle no one talked about. Yuri was the Salty's.

"I'm not," he told the older man fondly, "but you look like you might. Why don't you go in the back and sleep it off?"

Marta looked from the man to Ike, puzzled. "Sleep it off? But it's only three in the afternoon." Even though it was already dark outside, wasn't that a little early to be inebriated enough to need to sleep it off?

"Yuri got an early start, didn't you, Yuri?"

But Yuri made no answer. Slumped in his chair, his head thrown back against the padded cushion, the older man was snoring loudly. Ike smiled. "I love it when they listen to me." Making a choice, he selected a man closer to him. "When he wakes up, Bart, take him home. Don't let him drive."

"Is that really necessary? There's nothing to hit."

"Maybe not," he agreed. "But men have been known to freeze to death behind the wheels of their vehicles, either falling asleep or running out of gas. Better safe than sorry. Can't afford to lose a paying customer," he added when he saw the dubious look on her face. She'd probably be more comfortable with that explanation than thinking kindly of him, he decided. With a hand to her back, he ushered her toward the doorway that led to his quarters. "Let's go upstairs."

"Works fast, don't he?" She heard someone laugh.

Parka or not, Ike felt her back stiffen beneath his hand. "Like I said, they're bored."

She didn't like them alleviating their boredom at her expense. "As long as you know that nothing's going to happen."

"Whatever you say, darlin'."

If the stairs hadn't been narrow enough to prevent a sudden, abrupt turn, she would have walked right back out. But the width made it difficult to maneuver a turn with him at her back, and the moment that it took her to debate was enough to allow her to cool down. She kept walking.

Leaning so that his body unavoidably brushed ever so slightly against hers, Ike opened the door for her. "This is it."

"It," as applied to creatures and undefinable things, was an apt word for the premises. The quarters were exactly what she might have expected of a man who was accustomed to living on his own. Or of a place that a tornado had recently passed through. She judged that there were more things strewn around on the floor and every available surface than there were in the closets.

"Sorry," he mumbled, picking things up as he went and stuffing them under his arm. After a few attempts, they began to fall from the other side. He tossed the whole mess onto a sofa that already had too much on it. "I wasn't expecting to have anyone up here." He glanced toward the baby, knowing that Marta would point out that he'd expected to return with Celine. "Anyone who'd be critical, I mean."

Her eyes swept over the chaotic room. She would have understood the condition had the mess given the appearance of being fresh. After all, Ike had received not only one shock yesterday, but two. He'd lost his sister and gained a niece to care for.

But no one went through this many shirts in a day. This mess had a very long pedigree. She picked her way through to the table in the small kitchen. "I'm not here to be critical. I've seen pigsties before."

He laughed at her deadpan expression. The more he was around her, the more he found himself attracted. He supposed it was a matter of forbidden fruit being more tempting. That, and the fact that he'd already had a single taste of that fruit and knew firsthand that it was very sweet.

He shrugged out of his coat and began to toss it aside. Because she was here, he stopped and draped it over the back of a chair instead. "You do have a way of turning a phrase, darlin'."

She already knew that he shared these small quarters with Luc. Even cleaned up, there didn't look to be much room for a third occupant, however small.

Marta turned slowly around in the limited space. According to Sydney, beyond the main living area, which was a combination kitchen and living room, were two small bedrooms. She thought of the crib he'd told her was stored in his parents' attic. And they had just ordered several pieces of furniture for Celine. "Just where are you thinking of putting everything?"

"I'm not." He took Celine from her so that Marta could take off her parka. "Now that I have Celine, I thought I'd move into my folks' house."

She supposed that might make things easier all around. Certainly cut down on the risk of his losing the baby amid the mess. "They won't mind?"

A strange smile she couldn't quite read flirted with his mouth. "They haven't minded anything for a very long time." He saw the question in her eyes. "They've both been gone for almost fifteen years."

"Oh." That made him an orphan. "Fifteen years?" She thought of June. Hadn't he said she'd left Hades three years ago at eighteen? "That means that you—"

He nodded. "Practically raised Junie, yes, I know. Sure as hell—heck," Ike amended, glancing down at the baby he was holding against him, "hope I can do a better job with Celine."

He was making an effort not to curse in front of the baby. She wouldn't have thought that would occur to him. Marta wasn't aware of smiling as she took the baby back from him. "Well, at least you seem to be off to a good start. C'mon, let's see what else you know about babies."

The grin that spread across his mouth was nothing short of wicked. She felt something inside her threaten to unravel. "I know where they come from."

It was getting increasingly difficult to remain immune to his infectious smile, but she was trying her damnedest. "That doesn't count."

His eyes glinted with silent laughter. "It does in some books."

Mustering effort, she gave him a long, hard look she hoped put him in his place. "Not mine."

Ike merely inclined his head. His eyes told her he didn't believe her. "Duly noted, darlin'."

Darlin'. Even when he sounded as if he was being subdued, he'd weave that single word through and undermine whatever victory she'd thought she'd gained. The only way to deal with him was to try to focus on the matter at hand and shut out everything else.

"Sit down."

He did as she asked. "Why?"

She placed Celine on his lap. "Because I want to see you undress her."

His expression was bemused. "I'm accustomed to doing that with a somewhat older model."

"I'm sure you are." She suddenly realized that with one hand out of commission, there was no way this was going to work. "You also probably don't have to make sure their heads are properly propped up, either—unless you've gotten them drunk. Here, let me show you."

Sitting down beside him on the cluttered sofa, she removed the tiny parka from Celine one arm at a time, careful to switch hands so that Celine's head and back were supported at all times.

"To dress her, you just reverse the process." She paused, looking at his hand. "What are you going to do about tomorrow?"

"You could stay the night," Ike suggested. When she drew her brows together, he amended, "Or Luc could do it." Marta's expression was dubious. "I'll talk him through it."

"Guess that's going to have to do."

Standing up, she lifted Celine into her arms, patting the baby's bottom to soothe her. "Now do you know how to give her a bath?"

"I figure for the first year I'll just let the cat lick her," he quipped. "It's a joke, darlin'," he added when Marta pressed her lips together. There was no hint of a smile.

"That would be funny if I was sure it was. All right, why don't you fill up the sink, and I'll give her a bath?"

But crossing to the kitchen, she stopped. Dirty dishes were piled up high in the sink, like a disheveled, listing tower. At least there were no clothes in it, she thought sarcastically. "I see it's already filled up." Unable to hold her tongue any longer, she looked at him accusingly. "How can you live like this?"

He shrugged good-naturedly, turning on the water. "I manage."

"Obviously."

She had every intention of letting him take care

of the mess in the sink himself, she really did. But one-and-a-half dishes later, her impatience got the better of her. His washing with one hand was painstakingly slow. Watching him do it was even worse.

"Move out of the way. I'll wash the dishes and get the sink ready." Positioning the baby so that the transfer went smoothly, she handed Celine over to him. "Here, take your niece."

He tucked the baby against him. "Don't let her frighten you, Celine. She doesn't bite. She's really a very nice lady. She just likes to scare people off with her bark."

Marta struggled with a smile that wanted to surface as she looked over her shoulder at him. "Hasn't worked with you."

"No," he agreed. His smile split carefully crafted seams within her. "It hasn't."

She looked back at the sink, moving quickly. "I guess I'll just have to bark harder."

"If you like."

What she would like would be for him to stop using that tone of voice with her. The one she was certain he used on other women during seduction. "What makes you think I don't bite?"

He drew closer to her, watching in fascination as shadows from the overhead fixture played over her face. "Some things, a man just knows. Call it instinct."

Stacking a dish on the rack, she let out a short breath. "I call it overconfidence."

"We'll see."

She jumped when she felt his fingers along her neck. Swinging around, she almost bumped against Celine. "Don't do that."

The look in his eyes was innocent. And amused. He probably thought he had her number, she thought, annoyed. "The label was sticking out from the back of your sweater. I was just tucking it in."

She tossed her head, as if to shake off the feel of his hand. "I can tuck in my own label."

He merely smiled. "I'm sure you can."

To prevent the fluttering feeling in her stomach from growing to huge proportions, she directed her line of vision to the sink and the suds that surrounded her hands. Focusing was a struggle.

"Sorry about being late," Shayne said as he turned on the ignition. It was dark within the vehicle, but he'd seen her face clearly at Ike's. Marta looked exhausted. "So, how was it?"

Buckled in, Marta sank back into the seat, wondering how far she'd have to sink to outdistance the weariness that was clinging to her. She couldn't remember ever feeling this exhausted. It'd been a long time since she had taken care of a newborn. The years in between had made her forget how tiring it could be.

Or had she had more energy when she was younger? Certainly she'd had little else to focus on except the children she'd been asked to "mind."

Not only had she taken it upon herself to care for the baby, but every time Celine had fallen asleep, unable to endure chaos for more than five minutes at a stretch, Marta had straightened up Ike's living quarters. She'd done the latter despite Ike's rather vigorous protests.

"Tiring," she finally mumbled to Shayne.

He laughed softly, turning the radio on. Soft, soothing music from another era filled the interior. "Poor Marta, this is a hell of a way to spend a vacation," he commiserated.

She managed a smile, though she would have sworn that her face muscles, as tired as she, had lost the ability to function. "I don't mind. I like being busy."

It was true—she preferred it to inactivity. That way she didn't have too much time to dwell on a life that had gone nowhere. Oh, she was doing very well in her field, had the respect of her students and their parents to the degree that many of the parents specifically requested that she be their child's teacher.

But on a personal level, after Alex, everything within her had become as frozen as the terrain they were driving through.

That's why she had to keep busy.

"How's Ike taking to enforced fatherhood?" Shayne was asking.

She roused herself from her thoughts. "Better than I would have expected." She gave the devil his due. "I've only been around him a few hours, but he seems to really love that little girl."

That didn't surprise Shayne. He remembered the

way Ike had taken care of June. How he'd worried about her. And how hard he took her leaving town the way she had. Ike had never come right out and said how he'd felt, but it was still evident.

Shayne concentrated on the road, knowing how easy it was to get lost in the dark. He looked for familiar signs. "Ike's got a great capacity to love."

Marta laughed shortly. "So I hear."

"No, I mean that he's never had any woman say a single bad thing against him," Shayne said after a beat.

Right. "You're a man and he's your friend. You're supposed to say something like that." Men stuck up for one another. It was a given. Alex's friends had known he was seeing other women and they had all covered for him, making sure she didn't find out. Until she had.

"No, I'm supposed to envy something like that and I do," he told her honestly. "Ike hasn't been a choirboy since he was fourteen years old."

Shayne remembered envying that, too, at the time. When they were kids, growing up, Ike had always been the leader. As carefree as his own younger brother, Ben, had been. But beneath all the fun had been a man who could be counted on. That made the difference between Ike and Ben, he thought.

"He's had his share of women," Shayne continued, then laughed as he rethought his words. "Hell, he's just about had everyone's share of women. But not a one has ever bad-mouthed him after they've gone their separate ways. A lot felt free enough to call on him if they ever needed something." He looked at Marta, wanting to make her understand. "Ike's the kind of man people know they can count on for help."

Marta knew the signs. She'd been in this position before, when people had tried to fix her up with someone. The difference being, this time she knew the prospective candidate. "You wouldn't be trying to sell me on him, would you?"

Shayne shook his head. That hadn't been his intention. He just wanted her to be fair. "Ike sells himself. I'm just trying to make sure you don't keep slamming the door in his face before he has a chance to say hello."

Without meaning to, she ran the tip of her tongue along her lips. Remembering. "Oh, he's had a chance to say hello, all right."

Shayne thought it prudent not to smile, though he remembered what Sydney had told him about Marta mistakenly kissing Ike at the airport. He could imagine Ike hadn't been slow in reciprocating.

"Then I won't say any more." He paused a second. "Except to add that I've always felt that Ike could do with a really good woman in his life."

He *was* trying to sell Ike, Marta thought. Why? The man didn't lack for companionship. And anyway, she wasn't staying on. She was just visiting.

"I'm sure he feels he's doing fine just the way he is," she assured Shayne. "Besides, I'm only here for a couple of weeks. No offense, but this is a really harsh place to live.'' From everything Sydney had written, she knew that summers in Hades were no picnic either. Sydney was here because she was in love. But there'd never be anything like that to keep Marta here.

''That's the challenge of it.'' He looked relieved when he saw the lights of home. ''Nothing makes you feel more alive than a challenge, Marta.''

Chapter Ten

Marta had come to help Ike make his house more livable.

At least, that was the excuse she'd grasped at when Shayne had presented it to her, asking her if she wanted to join Sydney, the kids and him. It had been a while since the old LeBlanc house had been lived in, and Shayne had said there were things that were in desperate need of repair. Once Junie had moved out, Ike hadn't needed the space and had lost the inclination to fix it.

It seemed as good an excuse as any to hide behind. After several days of playing nanny to Celine while instructing Ike on the finer points of caring for an infant, Marta would have thought that she'd have had her fill of Ike LeBlanc.

She hadn't.

So, here she was, continuing to volunteer her services, all the while learning more and more about this man who had such a special place in the hearts of her best friend and her family.

Despite herself, and because of Celine, Marta was beginning to see Ike as something more than the two-dimensional man she'd first thought him to be. There was a kindness to him when he held the baby, and there was love in his eyes. It softened Marta's heart to watch him.

And, try as she might to deny it, there was something building between them. An attraction she couldn't seem to shake. An attraction that kept pulling her in. She was beginning to realize that chemistry was a great humbler. With hand outstretched and lightning emanating from its fingers, it summarily did away with noble ideals and principles.

But, chemistry or not, she insisted silently, if you knew what was behind a magic act, it took the magic away. And she knew what was behind Ike's magic act, at least where women were concerned. A smile that was empty, bedroom eyes that never went into the kitchen, or any other room where marriages endured. And a wicked mouth that spoke words to make a woman's heart skip a beat. Expedient words that were no doubt forgotten the instant they emerged.

Sure, he had a few good qualities, but that didn't change who he was: a man who seemed determined to make his way through the entire female population of Alaska before heading down to conquer the lower forty-nine.

Well, he wasn't going to hang her pelt from his cabin door. If she remembered that, his smiles wouldn't seem as sexy, his eyes as seductive. And his mouth...well, she just wouldn't look at his mouth, that's all. Or be anywhere within its reach.

It sounded like a plan to her. All she had to do was stick with it, she thought as Shayne parked the car.

It looked as if half of Hades had decided to show up.

"What's going on?" Marta raised her voice so that Sydney could hear her.

Sydney hooked her arm through Marta's, already drawing her toward the heart of the crowd. "Ike's moving in, remember?"

"Yes, I know. That's why we're here. But—" And then it penetrated. "Are they all here to—?"

"Help," Shayne supplied the last word for her. "Yes, they are. People in Hades tend to pitch in a lot. It's one of the nice things about living out here."

Probably the only nice thing, Marta thought, but she kept it to herself.

It wasn't hard for her to find Ike. He was the one in the middle of a crowd within the crowd. His crowd comprised solely women, both old and young. Why didn't that surprise her?

"Doesn't look as if he's particularly lacking for help," Marta murmured.

Sydney's hold on her arm tightened just a shade as she continued ushering her through the gathering. "You know how women are when they see a new baby. They cluster."

Why was Sydney so determined to make excuses for Ike? It wasn't as if she couldn't see for herself what was going on. "The fact that the new baby is in Ike's arms doesn't have anything to do with it, Sydney, and you know it."

"It has everything to do with it," Shayne interjected. Walking close to his wife, he made sure no one would jostle her. "They just want to help him."

Marta shook her head. "Well, with that much help, he certainly doesn't need mine."

Shayne looked at her pointedly. "I think he does."

Marta wanted to protest, and politely but firmly argue the point. But it was too late. Ike had already seen them. Holding Celine, he cut a path for himself and was walking toward them. The cluster of adoring females was left behind to meld into the crowd.

"Hi." The greeting was hearty, and he sounded almost relieved. "I didn't think you were coming." Nodding at Shayne, Ike paused to kiss Sydney's cheek.

"I'm surprised you even noticed we were missing." Marta hadn't meant to say that out loud. She knew how it had to sound. As if she was jealous. Nothing could be farther from the truth.

The quip only amused him. "I notice everything." Ike winked at her.

"So you said." Marta took a discreet deep breath, trying to still the flutter that insisted on rising up every time she was on the receiving end of his wink.

Shayne saw his chance and took it. Commandeering Ike, he nodded toward the baby. "Why don't one of you ladies take Celine while I see about putting that hand back into commission?"

Since she was closer, Marta took charge of Celine. "Being one-handed doesn't seem to be hindering him any," she murmured, not quite under her breath. The sound of Ike's amused laugh did nothing to restore her humor. But holding Celine did. "Hello, precious. I see he finally got the hang of dressing you right."

"Actually, that was Luc's doing." Ike's honesty surprised her. She would have expected him to take advantage of even a minor compliment. He held up his bandaged hand. "I still need practice." Celine cooed. "That's her way of saying she missed you." Ike raised his eyes to Marta's. "So did I."

Ike was getting used to seeing her come by every day to help with Celine. It had just been a matter of a few days, and now that he thought about it, it amazed him how quickly he'd become comfortable with the routine.

And how much he liked having her around.

Marta purposely glanced back at the cluster of

women he'd left behind when he'd approached them. Several were still looking his way.

"I sincerely doubt that."

Shayne placed himself between Marta and Ike. They could settle this later. "Let's get that looked at. I want to get this taken care of so you don't continue playing the invalid."

Ike led the way to the house. The back door was standing wide open. Several new appliances had been brought inside, replacing nonfunctioning ones—donations from some of the neighbors.

"And who's the one who insisted on playing doctor and bandaging me up this way when I said it was nothing?"

Shayne made no reply as he followed Ike into the old kitchen. For the moment, it was empty. As Ike sat down and drew his chair up to the table, Shayne placed his bag down and opened it.

He paused a second to look around. If he concentrated, he could almost hear Ike's father, his thick French accent making everything he said sound melodic. Even when he cursed. "Boy, being here brings back memories."

"It sure does, doesn't it?" Ike leaned back, wishing he could go back, even for the space of a day. But there were no return trips allowed. Good or bad, life just kept moving forward. He caught his friend's eye. "Remember when the weight of the world wasn't on our shoulders and the word *responsibility* was just something in a dictionary?"

"Quite frankly? No." To Shayne it felt as if he'd

always been in charge, always been the responsible one. That went doubly for Ike.

Taking out a pair of surgical scissors, Shayne began to cut away at the tape and gauze surrounding Ike's hand. "So, what do you think of her?"

Ike had been wondering when Shayne would get around to asking. "I like her."

Shayne carefully drew back the stained bandage and inspected the wound. "You never met a woman you didn't like."

"True." Ike thought a moment. From his vantage point, he thought he caught a glimpse of Marta walking up to the house. It was almost as cold inside as it was out. "She's a honey."

The wound was healing well. Shayne spared Ike a glance before applying a salve. "I've heard you use that term before."

The salve stung. Ike steeled himself. "Maybe not with so much feeling, though." He grinned as Shayne looked at him.

Shayne began rebandaging Ike's hand. This time around, he was only covering Ike's palm. His fingers would heal faster out in the open.

"You realize, of course, if you hurt her, I'll be forced to kill you. Nothing personal, you understand." Snipping off the bandage, he put the scissors down and reached for tape. "It's just that Sydney'll make me—unless, of course, she does it herself. You know the pregnancy hasn't stopped her from doing everything else. I'm probably going to have to sit on her until she delivers to keep her from flying. But nothing will stop Sydney if you toy with Marta's heart.''

"You don't have to worry, I'm not toying. I'm just being a willing pupil.''

Shayne thought it best to leave that alone. There wasn't a woman born who could teach Ike anything. If he thought that Marta could, then maybe there was something substantial brewing. He wasn't about to jeopardize it by asking any more questions.

Cutting off the end of the tape, he tucked it around Ike's palm. "There, how does that feel?''

"Better.'' Ike wiggled his fingers. Fiery red ants danced along his palm and fingers, zigzagging as they went. "Still stiff, though, and they kind of sting some.''

"That's going to take time. You're just lucky those weren't second- or third-degree you sustained.''

"I guess next time I'll just let your house burn down.''

Clearing away the old bandages, Shayne deposited them along with his instruments into a side compartment in his medical bag, then snapped the bag shut. He regarded Ike quietly. "So, you're really serious about this, taking care of Celine?''

Ike's eyes met his. "You know me better than to have to ask.''

"I suppose I do.'' Shayne just saw it as a big undertaking for a single man. He remembered how he'd felt when he brought Sara and Mac back to live with him after his ex-wife had died. Com-

pletely overwhelmed. And they at least knew how
to dress themselves. "But have you really thought
this through? What are you going to do with Celine
while you're working?"

"Nothing to think through. I'll bring her with
me." Ike stood up. "When she gets older, I'll hire
a housekeeper to watch her when I can't be
around." His words struck him, and he laughed.
"Can you picture me with a housekeeper?" He'd
always thought of himself as too freewheeling for
something so restrictive and upper-middle class as
a housekeeper. "Who'd ever have thought it?"

Shayne shook his head. They'd both come a long
way from the boys who'd sat at this table, waiting
for Ike's mother to serve them up an extra slice of
her famous apple pie. "Well, your housekeeper certainly won't lack for work. I'll guarantee that much.
I've seen the way you keep house."

"Not anymore. You should see it now. Marta
decided it needed a makeover. Every time she
comes over, she sighs dramatically and makes me
pick up after myself." He laughed, remembering
the amazed look on Luc's face when he walked in
after her first visit. "Jean Luc is still wandering
around in a daze."

Shayne knew he was exaggerating, but not by
much. "That might be your perfect solution," he
kidded. "Marry someone to watch Celine, keep
your house in running order and your boots under
one bed."

He grinned, playing along. "Three birds with one stone—worth thinking about."

But marriage wasn't for him. He didn't see himself sharing his life with one woman. It wasn't that he felt he had to sample everything there was to life, or be with every woman who crossed his path. He'd just never felt that special feeling he knew was necessary to make a union permanent. He loved all women, but he'd never been *in* love with any of them. He figured he never would be.

When he saw a strange look cross Shayne's face, Ike stopped talking and turned around. Marta was standing in the doorway. Celine was still in her arms.

It was part of Ike's charm to recover without missing a beat. "What can I do for you, darlin'?"

Marta shifted her hand from beneath the baby's bottom. The dampness was beginning to seep through the blanket. "You can tell me where the diapers are. Celine needs changing."

"Diapers..." His voice trailed off. Damn, he knew he'd forgotten something.

"They're at the Salty, aren't they?" It wasn't really a question, she could read his expression. Marta was beginning to read him rather well. Ike's nod was almost superfluous. "Well, unless you want to diaper this precious bottom in a pillowcase, provided you have one here, I suggest you go back and get a few." If he forgot the diapers, he probably forgot other things, too. "While you're at it—"

With a sigh, she shook her head. "Never mind, just take me with you."

He covered one of her hands with his bandaged one. "My pleasure, darlin', but this is so sudden—"

She shrugged him off. "Save your charm for someone who'll buy into it, LeBlanc." She looked at Celine. "I'll change her at the Salty and then get some things together." There was a knowing look in her eyes. "You probably didn't bring any of her formula with you, did you?"

He couldn't help the smug smile. "As a matter of fact, I did."

She lifted a careless shoulder, then let it fall again. "I guess even a monkey gets things right once in a while."

He inclined his head close to hers, as if to whisper in her ear. "Is it my imagination, or are you just a little testier than your usual self?"

She didn't like the fact that the feel of his breath along her skin made parts of her body contract and tighten. Liked even less the thought that he somehow knew the effect he was having on her. "It's your imagination. I'm just as testy now as I ever was."

He laughed. "You'd be the one to know, darlin'. All right." He turned to Shayne. "I'll leave you in charge of things. Tell everyone I appreciate all their help and that they can collect a drink on me at the Salty anytime they want to. This shouldn't take too long."

Ike glanced at Marta as he made the last promise. Maybe, if he was lucky, it would take a little longer than that. Her resistance surely did intrigue him. And he freely confessed that there was something almost mouthwatering about the woman. He could feel himself getting stirred just by looking at her.

Desire, always something he could summon or dismiss at will, had begun to nibble insistently away at him. He supposed it had something to do with the fact that she was so keen on putting him into the place she felt he belonged. That she was so set on resisting him.

Somehow, he was going to have to find a way to get her to put down that rapier she was wielding so well, long enough to get a little closer to her.

He figured that getting a little closer was about all he needed.

Following him up the stairs to the rooms above the nearly deserted saloon, Marta halted abruptly at the doorway. "Doesn't take you long, does it?"

He was halfway across the floor to where he'd put the package of diapers. "What do you mean?"

She stooped to pick up the shirt she'd seen him wearing yesterday. "I just straightened all this up yesterday." She draped the shirt over the back of the chair. The room wasn't as bad as it had been when she'd walked in several days ago—she doubted if that was possible—but it was definitely going in that direction. The line about changing a leopard's spots drifted through her mind.

Taking a diaper from the pack, Ike stifled a yawn. "It was a long night."

Marta lay Celine down on the sofa and began stripping off the old diaper. Ike handed her the new one. As she took it from him, she looked more closely at his face. He did look tired. Sympathy tugged at her.

"Did you get any sleep at all?"

Ike had gone without sleep before. But never for quite such altruistic reasons. These last few days had taken a great deal out of him, despite Marta's help. He shrugged away her query. "A little here, a little there. Might have been as much as ten minutes, total."

She believed him. She'd been in several foster homes with babies under a year old. Colicky babies, whose nights were endless and exhausting, filled with crying.

She applied the diaper quickly, then set Celine down on the floor in her infant seat. "Why don't I take Celine for a little while, and let you get a couple of hours' sleep?"

He thought of the people who had turned out to help fix up the old house. Good people who were generous with their time just because he needed them.

"While everyone else is at the house, working?" He shook his head. "That wouldn't go over too well. Besides, I couldn't do that."

She was surprised that he even thought of that.

Very carefully, she placed Celine into her infant

seat. Setting the seat on the floor, she rose to her feet and walked out of the small room. He followed her.

"I'm sure everyone would forgive you."

Taking her hand, he turned her around. "If I'm not back within a reasonable amount of time, they'll probably think I'm making love with you."

His eyes were soft, seductive and already making love to her. She shook off the thought as being ridiculous. Eyes didn't make love.

But his…

She cleared her throat. "Why, because every woman finds you irresistible?"

"No," he said quietly, his hand slowly moving up the length of her arm, "because I find you irresistible."

"You do." She tried to sound sarcastic, skeptical, but it was all she could manage just to force the words out of her mouth.

She had beautiful eyes, Ike thought. Beautiful features. Yearning poured, warm and silky, through his veins. "I do."

Marta tried to rally, but the stadium was woefully underpopulated. "Bull."

"Fact," he whispered in the same tone she used. "Just because you'd rather shoot me than look at me doesn't mean that I can't find you completely fascinating." With his good hand, Ike feathered his fingers through her hair, amazed at how soft it felt to his touch. "Completely breathtaking."

Marta tried not to swallow like some silly adolescent, but her throat suddenly felt so terribly dry. "For someone whose breath has been taken, you certainly seem to have enough to spare."

His smile was so compelling, she found it hard not to become lost in it.

"See, that's what I find so fascinating about you. You're not only beautiful, you've got a sharp mind to go along with that sharp tongue of yours." And Ike longed to feel that tongue entwined with his own. Longed to know her body, urgently pressed against his. Longed to hold her after it was over, comforting himself with the sound of her breathing. "And you're kind to boot."

"Kind?" Was he going to say something about her taking pity on his tortured soul and relieving his fevered anguish, or nauseating words to that effect? Marta tried to summon indignation, knowing it was her best defense against an assault that was taking surprising hold on her.

"Tending to a child for a man you loathe is kind in my book, darlin'."

She wished he wouldn't brush the back of his hand along her face that way. Wished that it didn't make her feel as if her knees were made out of ice cubes that had been left out too long. "I don't loathe you, I—"

"You what, darlin'?" he coaxed softly, his face somehow closer to hers than she remembered. "You what?"

Was that panic drumming through her? She wasn't supposed to feel panic. She was supposed to feel smug, superior. And immune. Definitely immune. What was going wrong?

She thought of Celine, and grasped at the lifeline before she went over the falls in a barrel made of paper. "I've got to go see about feeding her."

"I fed her before I brought her to the house," he told her. Was it possible? Was Buffy, the Vampire Slayer turning into a soft, seductive Juliet? "And you just changed her. So unless one of us is itching to give her spelling lessons, I'd say that for the moment, we've done all we can for her—and can leave her in her infant seat."

Her tongue darted out, moistening lips that refused to stay moist. "And do what?"

"Whatever comes to mind."

"And I suppose you already have some ideas." Was that her? Giving him straight lines? Lines that would lead to her downfall if she wasn't careful?

"A few." *Oh, more than a few,* Ike added silently, the intensity of his own desire surprising him.

Very lightly, he ran the tip of his finger along the outline of her lips and watched excitement flower in her eyes.

And roar in his veins.

Taking her into his arms, he lowered his head and kissed her.

And all the defenses Marta had so painstakingly erected within her began to shake and rattle like a house built on a gaping fault during an earthquake.

Chapter Eleven

Ike knew himself too well to think that what he was feeling was just something ordinary, that what was happening could be thought of as simply business as usual.

There was nothing usual about this.

The moment his kiss deepened, the moment he tasted her and his own erupting desire, Ike knew this was something he hadn't encountered before. That what she aroused within him was desire with a capital D, passion set up in glowing neon lights that could rival any dynamic sunset Alaska had to offer. There was something about this initial contact, with its hint of things not promised but nonetheless existent, that efficiently and completely set him on fire.

It was all he could do to keep from sinking to his knees in stunned wonder.

He'd never felt like this before. While the number of women he'd been with hadn't actually been legion, there'd been enough for him to know that this was different. That this woman was different.

And that he wanted her more than he'd ever wanted anyone or anything else in his life.

Marta dug her fingertips into his shoulders, trying to anchor herself. His kisses were soft, urgent, drugging. Each one was a little more so than the last. More wondrous, more intoxicating, more forceful.

More.

And she found herself welcoming it and wanting more.

So much more.

Maybe it was because she hadn't been with a man since Alex had left her life. She hadn't wanted anyone, had purposely made sure there wasn't anyone who could get this close to her ever again. Close enough to take her into his arms. Close enough to kiss her. Close enough to completely ignite all her resolve, all her good plans.

Ike had taken her fences and burned a hole right through them, giving him complete, unrestricted access to her. There were ashes all around her, and she didn't care. She'd think about that later.

Knowing only that she wanted desperately to get even closer to the heat, Marta rose up on the tips of her toes and wound her arms around his neck, her body cleaving to his.

She felt his arms embracing her, felt his mouth leaving her lips to anoint her jawline, her throat, her soul. Pulling her farther and farther into a vortex. Her pulse began to race as if trying to outrun the sensation. To outrun it and hurry back to the starting line where her common sense waited. But someone had erased the starting line.

She didn't care. Her heart rejoiced with a surge that overwhelmed her.

When his hands dipped beneath her sweater and cupped her breasts, Marta sucked in air. This was where she should call a halt to everything, her brain ordered.

But she didn't. Instead, she arched into his touch.

With that one small act, she surrendered to him. Became his prisoner.

His jailer, Ike realized, his mind barely able to form coherent thoughts. The only way he could have walked away now was if she pushed him away. She would have to be the one to call a halt to what was happening, because, on his own, he knew he couldn't.

That had never happened before.

No one enjoyed lovemaking as much as he did, but he'd always been able to hold back before, been prepared to stop at a moment's notice. That power wasn't within his grasp anymore.

He found himself completely unprepared for what was happening to him. And praying that she wouldn't suddenly change her mind.

Still, it was only fair to give her a chance to

stop—or continue. To know that what was happening *was* happening because she wanted it to, not because he was silently pressuring her, manipulating her.

Though his body begged him not to, he drew away. And looked at her face. "Marta?"

Had he called her darlin', she might have summoned the strength to pull away. Somehow found the energy to search for a mind that had suddenly vanished, taking her common sense hostage in the wake of the onslaught of his lips.

But he'd said her name and it had made all the difference in the world to her.

It softened her heart.

"Yes," she breathed. "And don't you forget it."

Her hands framing his face, Marta brought his lips back to hers. And destroyed any chance that this might end before it began.

Ike had less choice than a leaf being swept up in an autumn wind.

The urgency of his kisses increased as he drew her sweater away from her body. With one swift tug, he pulled it over her head and discarded it. In his eagerness, he'd almost tossed the garment into the fireplace and the dying fire that graced the hearth.

Eager. That was the only way he could begin to describe what he was feeling. The sensations ricocheting through him took him entirely by surprise. He couldn't remember ever experiencing this degree of excitement coursing through his body, except, perhaps, for the first time.

This was like the first time.

The only thing was, he wasn't an inexperienced fourteen-year-old boy anymore. He was a man who had known women. Known that there was no mystery to them, only degrees of intensity.

But there was a mystery now. A mystery as to why this one small woman with her sharp tongue and perfect mouth could undermine him so. Could make him feel so completely at the mercy of his passions. A mystery as to why he felt like a clumsy schoolboy with her.

He wanted this to be spectacular for her, to be memorable beyond all other times that she might have had and would have to come.

He wanted—

Only her.

His arms tightened around Marta almost possessively as his lips raced along her face, her chin, the swell just above her bra. He hardly knew himself.

Marta's lungs seemed to be incapable of holding more than a thimbleful of air. Why else was she gasping for breath when all she was doing was standing still?

That was just it, she wasn't standing still. She was vibrating. Vibrating so hard that if it were any faster, she was in danger of slipping into another dimension entirely.

Her head was whirling and her body all but screaming out for him. Not for release, not for fulfillment, but for him. For Ike. For the culmination of everything his kisses, his touches, silently promised her.

She knew he couldn't possibly live up to it, no man could, but she didn't care. She wanted whatever it was that he could give her. And wanted it now, before she found herself exploding in anticipation.

Or before reason came to ruin everything.

Her skin tingled as she felt her jeans drop from her body. Somewhere along the line in between, although she couldn't pinpoint when, she'd stepped out of her boots, standing on the toe of one while drawing her foot out of it, then reversing the process.

And once his lips left hers, once they began forging trails along her throat, her shoulders, her breasts, she wasn't capable of performing even the simplest of tasks. That would take some semblance of a thought process and all her thoughts were centered on the delicious sensations urgently chasing one another through her body.

Belatedly, just before she sank into complete euphoric oblivion, Marta realized she must seem like a submissive, limp rag doll to him. Receiving when she should have been sending. Taking when she should have been giving.

The word *survive* screamed through her head.

She hadn't managed to survive by submitting. By being passive. Passive people were soon forgotten, left behind.

Abandoned.

The single word rose up in front of her closed eyes, slicing through the hot haze that enveloped her.

She'd been abandoned, not once, not twice, but so many different times by so many people who had marched through her life. By families. And a lover.

Abandoned.

The word echoed in her brain, galvanizing her.

Not this time.

It was, Ike thought, as if someone had suddenly set a match not to a fuse, but to the dynamite stick itself. Marta's body tensed against his, snapped to attention. Before he could ask her what was wrong, he suddenly found himself under siege.

Marta splayed her fingers over his chest, coming in contact with the buttons on his shirt. Trying to still the shaking within her, she quickly undid them, tugging his shirt out of his jeans.

As she pulled it from his shoulders, Ike inclined his head, grazing her neck with his lips. It just increased the wild sensations battering her body. She felt like a driven woman, afraid that if she stopped, all this would abruptly fade away. End. She couldn't let that happen, not yet.

The level of her response overwhelmed him. He wanted to take her here, now, this second, without a moment's hesitation.

But this was so fierce, so sudden, that he had to be sure this was what she wanted. His heart pounding harder than a miner's jackhammer, he struggled to do the decent thing. To give her an opportunity to say no even though everything she was doing to him screamed yes.

Though he knew he might live to regret it, Ike caught her hand just as she began to undo the snap on his jeans. She looked at him with dazed confusion in her eyes.

"Are you sure?"

Her throat suddenly felt as if it had been dragged behind a galloping mustang for twenty miles, then cut loose. She stiffened. "A little late to be asking that, isn't it?"

"Never too late," he whispered against her hair, breathing in the scent of her. Because she'd stiffened, Ike drew back, searching her eyes. The anger caught him off guard.

Marta felt completely shaken. She'd been tottering on the brink, ready to throw not only caution but everything else away because he'd undone her so, and the bastard was obviously calm enough to walk away from her. She'd had less than no effect on him.

She jerked free of his hand, looking for her sweater. What had he done with it? "So you can just turn this off? Like some damn faucet?"

Like the survivor of a hurricane, unceremoniously dumped on the ground after a whirlwind ride, Ike could only stare at her. He felt as if his brain had been numbed. "What?"

How dare he look at her as if she were talking

some foreign language? Marta saw her sweater next to the fireplace and snatched it up. "Did you even feel anything?"

Crossing to her, he turned her around to face him. "They haven't come up with the words yet to describe what I'm feeling."

"Right." She jammed her arms through her sweater and started to pull it over her head. "That's why you can just stop at the drop of a hat."

Catching her sweater, he pulled it back up over her head. "Not at the drop of a hat. At your word."

Now what did he think he was doing, playing musical sweaters? She tried to reclaim it, but he held the sweater high over his head. Incensed, she glared at him. "My word?"

He threw the sweater aside. When she started to go for it again, he grabbed her wrist and held her in place. Ike struggled to control a temper that rarely surfaced. She was going to listen to him, not storm out.

"If you don't want this to go further, then it won't. It'll stop here and now." Because she wasn't looking at him, he took her chin and gently but firmly directed her eyes toward him. He wasn't going to let her think she was just a number, or a warm body. He didn't operate that way to begin with, and never less than now. "I'll probably self-destruct, and Jean Luc's going to find himself Celine's guardian." He swept back her hair from her eyes. He'd never seen green so brilliant before.

"But I won't force you, and I won't force myself on you."

"Force me," Marta echoed in disbelief, struggling to make sense out of what he was saying. He was doing this for her? "Is that what you think is happening here?"

Ike searched her eyes again. The fire was abating, but there was still doubt there. Doubt he had no idea how to erase. He only knew that he wanted to. "That's what I want to know."

"And if I said stop—?"

"Then it's stopped," he answered, his voice thick with feeling.

It took everything he had not to run his hands up along her bare arms, not to draw her close to him and seal his mouth to hers, abandoning all conversation. But he had a feeling that somehow this was about abandonment. He didn't want her to feel as if her needs, her feelings, were being left abandoned while he merely satisfied himself with her and went on.

"For me." Skepticism scratched at Marta, warring with feelings for which she knew she had no basis. There was no reason to believe that this man burned more brightly when the lights were out, that he wasn't at bottom thinking only of himself. That he wasn't trying to confuse her.

That all this wasn't just for effect.

And yet...

"For you," he answered softly. Ike touched her

face, his palm caressing her cheek. "It's not any good if you don't want it as much as I do."

Marta could feel her body quickening, her loins yearning. He was good, she thought. Very, very good. No matter how much she might want, on some other level, to hang onto her anger, she was outnumbered. Because she had thrown her lot in with his.

"Then it's good," she whispered, her lips temptingly close to his, her meaning clear. "Because I *do* want it as much as you do." *Maybe more.* At the very least, she was meeting him on this misty battlefield as an equal partner. And if there were regrets for being so honest, she would deal with them later. Now wasn't the time for them.

It was all Ike wanted to hear.

His mouth covered hers, doing away with the need for any more talk, any more soul-searching. All that could be sorted out later, when he was more able to reason. The slight break had only caused his desire to surge forward.

The white lacy underwear Marta wore, which had turned him on so much, quickly became superfluous layers. He tried not to be rough as he pulled them from her and discarded the flimsy garments on the floor. If things were different, if urgency's rapier had been just a little less pointed, he could have dallied, taken his time. Drawn them from her inch by inch, and excited them both.

But he was miles past that sort of foreplay. Needs

were battering urgently at him, pleading for release. It was all he could do to move as slowly as he did.

His own clothing followed a moment later.

Divested of barriers, their bodies sealed against one another like two lips pressed together. Heat surged from each of them, mingling, exchanging, fueling.

She made his head spin.

Kissing her over and over again, unable to sate himself, his hunger for her growing, Ike lowered her to the floor. To the warm, dark bearskin rug that had once been such a source of pride and storytelling for his grandfather. His body pulsing, he raced his mouth over her body, kissing, teasing, suckling. Determined to know every inch of her. Arousing himself almost past the point of endurance.

The rug felt soft beneath Marta's back as she sank deeper and deeper into it. Deeper and deeper into the swirling light show that Ike was creating for her sole pleasure. His mouth was making her insane with each pass over her body.

Marta moved urgently against him, absorbing each sensation as it burst upon her, forgetting her vows to reciprocate the favor and drive him as crazy as he was making her. Forgetting her promise never to allow any man to possess her so completely that she lost all sense of time, all sense of direction.

She had lost it now.

There was only a kaleidoscope of sensations that

repeatedly collided within her, making rainbows in the snow.

She wanted, so badly, to murmur words of endearment to him, to tell him what she was feeling. To share not only her body, but her soul with him.

She knew she couldn't, and it was the only thing that marred the moment for her. All her life, she'd looked for love in all the wrong places, given it to the wrong people only to have it thrown back at her, unused, unwanted. She wouldn't let it happen again. Would never say the words again.

No matter how much she wanted to.

This was almost beyond human endurance. If they gave medals for this, Ike would be at the head of the list. Maybe even be up for a Nobel prize. But even men with iron resolve had their limits, and he knew he couldn't hold himself back any longer. Her body was moving too eagerly against his—rubbing, arching, offering. He couldn't continue to refuse the gift, to hold himself in check while he explored and memorized every part of her. It just wasn't possible. The demands that were slamming into him with the force of a derailed freighter couldn't be denied any longer.

Invoking almost superhuman strength, he struggled mightily for just half a second more.

"Look at me," he told her hoarsely.

Dazed, Marta realized that her eyes were squeezed tightly shut. With effort, she forced her lids open, trying to focus.

Her pupils were huge, dilated. Ike felt something in his chest tightening at the sight of her.

''I want you to look at me,'' he repeated to her. ''When I take you, I don't want you to remember any other man, to think of any other man making love with you, but me.''

Marta's mouth curved then in a half smile she would have sworn she didn't have the energy to form. ''Branding me?''

''Wanting you.'' The words whispered along her skin, teasing her, arousing her. Making her his, even when she knew it was foolish to let them.

With his eyes holding hers and his palms pressed firmly against hers, fingers linked, Ike slowly lowered himself into her.

He caught his breath as he felt her sheathing him, tightening as the rhythm took hold. Rhythm that passed from him to her.

Or maybe it was the other way around. Ike couldn't say for sure. All he knew was that it was there, and that it caught him up firmly in its grasp as she moved with him. At first slowly, as if she were lost in the wonder of the joining, and then faster and faster, until there was nothing left but to ride to the top of an ever-rising summit, taking it, conquering it.

And being conquered.

He tasted her muffled cry within his mouth, along his tongue, and his heart quickened. He hadn't reached the final crest by himself.

Satisfaction drenched him, mingling with the perspiration between their sealed bodies. Having her there with him, purged and exhausted, made it all the sweeter.

With the last of his quickly ebbing strength, he gathered her to him and held her close, comforted by the beat of her heart. The rhythm matched his own.

Just as the rhythm of her lovemaking had.

Ike buried his face in her hair, breathing in the fragrance. Content to remain this way for a very long time.

Wishing he could.

The next moment, a loud knock on the door shattered all hope of that.

Chapter Twelve

"Ike, are you in there? Ike, it's Shayne."

Springing up from the floor, tense, alert, Ike grabbed Marta's hand and quickly pulled her to her feet. There was no time to notice the graceful curves he had been memorizing with his hands, no time to drink in how simply beautiful she was, no time to consciously realize that even now, spent and under siege, he wanted her all over again. They had a very immediate problem on their hands.

With an economy of movement, he scooped up her clothing and shoved it into her arms, along with her boots. Marta clasped them to her, as Ike silently pointed to the other room where the baby was. His message was clear.

Marta fled and closed the door behind her.

Grabbing his underwear, fervently hoping he'd get an opportunity to put them on before he left the building, Ike pulled on his jeans. He'd managed to throw on his shirt and finish buttoning it as he heard Shayne walking into the apartment. He was going to have to remember to start locking that door.

"Ike?"

"In here," he called, careful not to sound winded. Robbed of the chance to savor the aftermath, he still hadn't caught his breath from making love with Marta. Having to get dressed in under three seconds didn't help any.

Shayne stuck his head into the room. He raised his brow. "So you *are* here. I saw your car in the garage, but I thought when you didn't answer at first that—" He stopped dead, looking at Ike's bare feet. His socks were crumpled on the floor, one here, one there, with Ike's boots lying on their side in between. "Why are your boots off?"

He was just grateful that he'd managed to get his clothes on in time. Ike said the first thing that came to mind.

"Rock." As if to prove that was what he'd been about, he tipped a boot over, shaking it. It would have helped if there'd been something inside to come falling out.

Shayne looked at him skeptically. "In both boots?"

Having put his socks back on, Ike began to pull on his boots. He looked completely unfazed, as if he'd just been caught wading in a spring in the middle of summer.

"So now you're an expert on rocks and boots, as well as the health and well-being of this tiny, thriving community?"

Shayne eyed him. He knew that tone, recognized that look. Both telltale signs that Ike had been with a woman. But there was something else, something more. If he didn't know any better, Shayne would have said that Ike was a little nervous. But that didn't make sense. Ike was never nervous about his dalliances. They were as natural as the long six-month Alaskan nights.

Something was up.

As if in answer to his unspoken question, the door behind Ike opened.

Shayne didn't know if he was surprised to see Marta standing there, or if he'd actually been expecting it. In either case, he certainly had something to tell Sydney when he got back.

Marta had no idea why she felt so nervous. It wasn't as if she'd done anything awful, or even anything that was anyone's business but her own. And Ike had even gone out of his way to cover for her.

Why had he? It seemed unusually gallant.

The question, for now, was going to have to go unexamined.

Forcing a breeziness into her expression, she greeted Shayne with a nod before looking at Ike. She was almost grateful for this opportunity to play-act. It allowed her to try to pull herself together. She had absolutely no idea what to say to Ike about what had just happened. Whether to ignore it, excuse it, or forbid him to ever mention it to anyone—even her.

None of the choices included savoring it. Because Marta knew that would be a very fatal mistake on her part. If she savored it, she might make more of it than was meant to be.

"Well, I put Celine down. I don't know how long she'll be asleep." Hoping he couldn't hear how hard her heart was hammering, she swept her eyes toward Shayne, offering him a wide, surprised smile. "I didn't hear you come in."

Shayne merely inclined his head. "I'll try to be louder next time." Not sure how successful he was at keeping the grin from his face, he turned away from them and pretended to glance toward the window.

His other boot on, Ike rose to his feet. He looked at Marta pointedly. "Guess it was just my imagination, darlin'."

Confused, wondering if she'd just missed a cue, she could only stare at him. "About what?"

"About the rock in my boots." Laughing, he turned toward Shayne to explain. "I started taking them off, and she thought I was getting ready for something else." There was no need for the wink; his implication was crystal clear.

Marta didn't know whether to be indignant at what he was saying, or grateful for the camouflage.

It still amazed her that he wasn't trying to brag in some subtle way about what had just happened.

"I wouldn't have the time for that, as lovely as your houseguest is." He purposely swept his eyes over her slowly.

Marta could almost feel him touching her, and it took all she had not to let herself react.

"Not with everything I have to do at the moment," Ike was saying. He looked at Shayne. "What are you doing here, anyway?"

He'd been sent out as a one-man search party. "People were beginning to wonder where you disappeared to."

"We told you that we were coming here to change Celine's diaper and get some more of her things," Marta reminded him. "Don't you remember?"

Shayne merely shrugged. Sydney had become concerned about them after a while. Sometimes it was less difficult acquiescing to a pregnant woman's wishes than reasoning with her. "Seemed like a long time to change a diaper, that's all."

Ike began piling the packages of diapers onto the table, preparing them for transport. He kept his back to Shayne. The man read him too damn easily.

"Well, then Celine was hungry and one thing just led to another," Ike tossed off carelessly. He glanced at Shayne over his shoulder. "You know how it is."

Shayne's smile widened. "Yes, I know exactly how it is." As if she knew she was the topic under discussion, Celine began crying in the other room. "Looks like the nap didn't last very long." He zipped up his parka. "Well, if everything's all right, I'll see you both back at your house."

Marta gratefully took that as a cue to leave the room and see to the baby.

"By the way—" Shayne stopped by Ike, lowering his voice "—your shirt buttons aren't aligned." There was laughter in his eyes as he walked out of the room.

Muttering under his breath, Ike quickly remedied the problem.

"What did he say?" Marta asked. Drawn by the sound of the front door closing, she returned to the room, holding Celine.

Ike thought fast. He figured she wouldn't appreciate learning of Shayne's keen eyesight. "Just that he thought he heard Alonso say that the electricity would be turned on by nightfall," he said, referring to Alonso MacTavish, Hades's one-man utility company.

She hadn't thought of that. She'd just assumed that the basic necessities such as water, electricity and telephone were in working order. This was the wrong place to make those kind of assumptions, she reminded herself. "Otherwise what?"

He went into the kitchen to pack up the cans of formula they'd recently purchased. Marta followed him. "Otherwise, Celine and I either spend the night in the living room in front of a roaring fire the way our pioneering forefathers and foremothers did—'' he grinned ''—or we spend another night here.''

Desperately trying to avoid a lull in the conversation that would allow him to redirect it, she asked, ''What are you going to do?''

''Not talk about trivial things right now.'' Finished, he closed the cardboard box. ''Either way is fine,'' he told her, answering her question.

Ike looked at her, unable to read the message in her eyes. Was she upset because Shayne had come when he did, or was she relieved? Relieved because it gave her an excuse to run from Ike.

One thing was sure, he'd never had so many questions regarding a woman before. He placed a hand on each of her arms. ''About what just happened here, I don't want you to think—''

Holding Celine closer, she shrugged and stepped back. ''Don't worry, I'm not. I'm not thinking about it at all.'' She walked back into the other room. ''And I'm certainly not going to discuss it with you.''

For a second, he stood in the kitchen, undecided. It was, he supposed, what every man wanted to hear after a casual liaison, even one that had been as passionate as this one had been. That the woman wasn't interested in dwelling on it and that she was shrugging it off as if it were just another daily occurrence, like answering the telephone or washing the dishes.

There were a great many men who would have envied him being in this position. But he wasn't quite sure if he numbered among them. Because beneath everything else was the small, slowly developing feeling that this hadn't been just a casual liaison. Not for her. And just possibly, not for him.

But for now, and for simplicity's sake, he decided to back away from the subject until he had more time to explore it. And more wits about him. At the moment, he was still just a little fuzzy around the edges about the whole thing. Besides, there was no telling who they'd send next if he and Marta didn't get back soon.

With a half shrug, Ike let it pass. "Whatever you say."

Whatever you say. He said it so casually, so carelessly. As if it didn't matter to him one way or another.

His response just told her that she was right. The sex had been spectacular, but it was just that—sex. There'd been no feelings involved for him other than the normal programmed response. Press button *A* and *B* will happen. It meant nothing more to him.

Now, how did she get it to mean nothing to her?

"You've been avoiding us."

Marta looked up from the wall in Ike's house that she'd been patching. The huge hole in it was now filled with wire and plaster. An enormous amount of plaster. She was still trying to smooth it all out.

Belatedly, she realized her mistake and lowered her eyes back to the plaster mix. Looking into his eyes was the closest thing to a fatal mistake she'd ever come across.

The man's eyes should be listed with the local police department.

"I've been working."

Crossing his legs, Ike lowered himself onto the floor beside her. He'd been watching her for the better part of the afternoon after they'd returned, usually with an entire room between them. Telling himself that it was really better this way. To put as much distance between himself and the lady, as well as the "incident," as possible. The lady didn't have *casual* written about her. Making love with Marta meant something beyond just the physical gratification, no matter what she might maintain to the contrary. It was the first step to commitment— to home and hearth and all the trimmings that went along with it.

The last thing he needed right now was another permanent relationship in his life. He'd already signed on for one that would last the next eighteen years, if not longer. The smartest thing he could do would be to steer clear of Marta Jensen for the remainder of her visit to Hades, and be grateful that she was making things easy for him.

Wisdom and logic didn't seem to be making much headway with him today.

As for making things easy for him, if she were doing that, she wouldn't be preying on his mind like this all afternoon. Wouldn't have such an iron grip on his thoughts when there was so much else to commandeer his attention.

"You've been avoiding us," he repeated. "And frankly, Celine is getting a little hurt by it." He nodded toward the baby, lying peacefully in her newly purchased layette, while all around her activity hummed like a swarm of summer bees gathering honey.

"Celine," Marta repeated, fighting off the urge to smile. Why was she smiling when he'd all but said, *Here're your walking papers?* And after shoving the papers into her hands, what did he want from her now?

He nodded. "You know how women are. Their feelings get hurt real easily."

What was it about his voice that sounded so seductive? Knowing everything she did, feeling the way she did, why did she find herself feeling as if she were a package whose wrapping was coming undone because the glue was melting? "And you're speaking as an expert."

Ike grinned. "Bona fide, born and bred." He watched as she spread yet another layer of plaster on top of the others. There'd be no drafts sneaking in through here, he thought, amused, no matter how cold it was outside.

"How many women's feelings have you hurt?"

She was trying too hard to sound like she didn't care, and it gave her away. "By last count?" he asked teasingly, playing along.

Her eyes narrowed as she looked at him. "By any count you want, as long as it's accurate."

He reassessed her expression and realized that this was too serious to tease about. "None."

Marta was tired of being told that he was close to being fitted for his wings as a saintly lover. "Oh, yes, the fable about the wandering lover with the heart of gold." Scooping up more plaster on her trowel, she slathered it onto the wall. "Sorry, I forgot about that."

"My guess is that what you should concentrate on forgetting about is the guy who hurt you."

Angry, she shoved the trowel hard against the wall, smoothing the residue out with a vengeance. "Don't you have someone else to charm, or some pollen to spread?"

"I'm afraid I'm all tapped out. I used up my supply for the day." Because she wouldn't turn around, he took the trowel out of her hands.

Sparks all but flew from her eyes as she glared at him. "I need that."

He held it just out of her reach. "You'll get it back once you hear me out."

"You might not be aware of it, but it's impossible to be anywhere around you and not hear you out." Wrapping what was left of her dignity tightly around her, Marta rose to her feet and dusted her hands off on her jeans. "Maybe you'd like to finish that yourself."

With that, she turned on her heel and walked off.

"If you ask me, the lady just put you in your place, cousin."

Feeling out of sorts, Ike didn't even bother turning around to spare Luc a glance. He wasn't accustomed to feeling this way. Wasn't accustomed to not knowing which end was up. Though his easygoing manner belied it, he was always the one in charge, the one who knew exactly where things were headed. Right now, he didn't have a clue as to which way things were going, or even how he wanted them to go.

All he knew was that the lady mixed him up something awful.

"No one asked you." He turned, thrusting the trowel at him. "Here, make yourself useful."

Luc looked at him closely. And then a grin sprouted, growing quickly until it encompassed his genial face. "Well, I'll be damned."

He couldn't quite read the look of sudden awareness in his cousin's blue eyes. "That's a matter of opinion."

"She's gotten to you, hasn't she?"

Ike's dark brown eyes narrowed. He didn't need to be ribbed right now, or to have his rather inexperienced cousin, who had only had one girl in his life, suddenly making judgments on him. "On the other hand, you just might be damned. And in the very near future, too."

Luc slapped him on the back, clearly enjoying himself. "I never thought I'd see the day when you couldn't handle a woman."

"And you never will." Following the path Marta had created before him, Ike walked away.

Twilight had long since arrived on the scene, ushering in the darkness long before it was due. It made no difference to the people gathered within Ike's house. They continued what they were about, determined to see it to its conclusion, no matter what the task.

It amazed Marta how doggedly everyone seemed to work. Doggedly and happily. Good-natured ribbing went right along with serious concentration. And through it all was woven the laughter and sometimes the shrieks of playing children.

She'd long since decided that communities such as these existed only in books found in the juvenile section of the library. She'd convinced herself while she was growing up and yearning for a place like this, that it was pure fantasy.

But there were places where fantasy met reality, and this seemed to be one of them.

She'd observed people going out of their way for one another here. A cynic might have said that they had to, or die in isolation, but Marta could see that there was more to it than that. The people who carved a life for themselves out of this frozen terrain had large, open hearts that reached out to one another. That cared about one another.

And about strangers.

"You're smiling."

Startled, Marta realized she'd been caught daydreaming. She turned around to see that Sydney had come up behind her.

"I would have thought you'd be too exhausted to smile. We worked you pretty hard today." Sydney had seen Marta join in on no less than three separate projects over the course of the day. It gave her hope that Marta might very well become one of them eventually.

"I don't mind hard work. I never have." She sighed, shaking her head as she watched three men working to put the finishing touches on what had been, ten hours ago, a crumbling staircase. "You know, when I was very young, I had this fantasy about being part of a family. About having people who cared about me." Marta knew she wasn't saying anything that she hadn't shared with Sydney before, but somehow she needed to say it now. "Not just fed me and made sure I had clothes on my back, but were there for me when I needed them."

But it had only been that—a fantasy. She'd never managed to be placed with a family who had any interest in keeping her past the time they had signed on for. Nobody had wanted her to be part of their family.

She was getting maudlin, Marta thought, annoyed with herself. That was due in part to Ike. If he hadn't touched emotions that she'd kept locked away so tightly, the rest might not have broken free.

She turned to Sydney. "I think I'm beginning to see why you like it so much here. Having good people like this around you is more important that having a three-hundred-channel satellite dish or fifteen different restaurants to choose from in a three-mile radius.''

Moved, Sydney slipped her arm around Marta's shoulders. ''I don't know about the fifteen different restaurants, but Rick Sellars and his family have a satellite dish. Reception's not all that great yet, they tell me, but we'll get there.'' Giving her friend a fond squeeze, she inclined her head against Marta's. ''We haven't been left behind in the nineteenth century, no matter how much it might seem that way at times.''

Marta smiled ruefully. ''I guess I was just being critical when I first got here because I missed you so much, and subconsciously I just wanted to convince you to come back with me.'' She looked down at Sydney's swollen abdomen, a testimony not just to her physical state, but to her emotional one as well. Sydney loved and was loved. And Marta was happy for her. ''As if you ever would.''

Sydney looked around at all the people she had come to think of as friends. All the people she had come to care about. ''Well, if Shayne and the kids wanted to leave, I'd go,'' Sydney told her, but there was a touch of reluctance in her voice. ''But I have to admit, I'd really miss living here. I think we've all put in a very full day. Do you want to come home with us, or stay on? I'm sure that Ike can bring you home if you want to finish something up.''

Sydney had purposely used the vague term *something*, allowing Marta her privacy. It wasn't work Sydney was thinking of. Shayne had told her about nearly walking in on the two of them. She couldn't have been happier.

But the last thing Marta wanted right now was to be alone with Ike, especially after this morning. "No, I'll come home with you. You're the one I came to visit, not Ike. I've spent more time with him—"

"All for a good cause," Sydney reminded her. "You were helping him learn his way around the baby."

If Marta hadn't been around, then Sydney would have been more than happy to volunteer her services to him. But her attention was already divided up enough for any two people. Having Marta here to help her out, even for a short while, was a blessing.

Marta thought of the women she'd seen clustered around Ike when they'd first arrived this morning. "He's got more than enough help, I'm sure."

She frowned as she heard what sounded like a high-pitched siren. That was a city noise, something she associated with ambulances and police cars, neither of which were in Hades. It had to be something else. She looked at Sydney. "What's that?"

Sydney paled slightly. The siren went off infrequently, but every time she heard it, chills ran up and down her spine. She hated the sound of it. Scanning the area, she saw Shayne, but didn't man-

age to make eye contact. He was striding toward
Ike. The latter was motioning toward a number of
other men gathering near the door.

Marta caught Sydney's arm, drawing her attention back to her. "Sydney, what is it?"

"Someone called in a fire." She felt as if her
heart was in her throat as she said it. Scrambling to
their feet, Mac and Sara came running toward her.

"Mommy, can we go see it? Can we?"

"Is Dad going?" Mac asked excitedly.

"Yes, he's going, and no, we're not going to go
see it. We're going to go home and wait for him
until he gets back."

"Back?" Marta echoed. "Back from where?
You told me Hades doesn't have a fire department."

"We don't." Sydney pressed Sara close to her.
"We have volunteers."

Several men were rushing past them to pile into
their vehicles and head for the source of the call.

Impulse seized her. Unable and unwilling to hang
back when there might be an emergency, Marta
grabbed her parka from the back of the chair where
she'd left it.

Stunned, Sydney stared after her. "Marta, where
are you going?"

"You said the town used volunteers, right?" she
called back over her shoulder. "Well, I'm volunteering."

The next minute, she hurried out the door.

Chapter Thirteen

Moving quickly, Marta found herself colliding with Ike the moment she set foot outside the door. Surprised, he grabbed her by the arm to steady her, as Marta caught her breath.

As if of one mind, they asked in unison, "Where are you going?"

"With you," Marta said, just as Ike answered, "To talk to you."

"Why?" Again they asked in unison.

Marta held up her hand to stop him from saying anything else. If this continued, they'd wind up going nowhere quickly. "You first."

"I wanted to ask you to take Celine home with you. There's no telling how long I'll be gone." Chagrin, as well as cold, colored his cheeks. "I forgot about her for a second when the alarm sounded.'' That said, he began moving away from Marta toward his car.

But Marta caught his sleeve, demanding his attention. ''Sydney can take her home. I'm going with you.''

Even if she hadn't been holding onto his sleeve, her words would have stopped Ike in his tracks. ''You're what?''

''Going with you,'' Marta enunciated slowly, raising her voice above the noise.

Was she out of her mind? ''This isn't some clambake we're going to.'' Deftly, he removed her hand from his sleeve. ''It's a fire, and I'm wasting precious time standing here talking about it.'' Glancing behind him, he saw that Shayne had already left. On top of everything else, Shayne had accepted the post of volunteer fire chief. Ike didn't like leaving him without backup.

''Then don't waste any more.'' Turning, Marta saw Sydney approaching them. ''Watch Celine for us,'' she called out to her.

''Don't worry about her,'' Sydney told them, raising her voice. ''I'll take her home with the children.''

That settled, Marta turned around, only to discover that Ike had already left. Stifling an unflattering oath about his immediate biological debt to the animal kingdom, Marta hurried to where she knew he'd left his vehicle parked.

He was starting up the Jeep. She'd caught up to him just in time.

It wasn't until after she flung herself into the passenger seat that Marta realized she'd used the word "us" in making her request of Sydney. Us. As if Celine were hers as well as Ike's. As if there were some sort of relationship between them instead of just a temporary, passionate coupling.

She hoped Sydney hadn't picked up on it.

Just a slip of the tongue, Marta comforted herself, nothing more. It didn't mean that she was actually beginning to think of Celine as hers in any fashion. A few random diaperings and feedings did not form any sort of lasting bond. She, more than anyone else, knew that. Hadn't she been in enough homes to learn that? Helped with enough babies who would never even suspect she'd been part of their lives for a short interim of time?

They weren't moving. She looked quizzically at Ike, waiting. "I think you'll make better time if you move that shiny stick back to the letter *D*.

He let the sarcasm go. Ike shifted in his seat, looking at her. What the hell was she trying to prove? "I'm only going to say this once. Get out of the car."

She responded by buckling up. "Okay, you've said it, now let's go."

He had no idea what to make of her behavior, and had no time to try. The car began to vibrate, protesting being left in neutral. "Get out of the car," he repeated a little more firmly.

"Going back on your word?" She looked at him innocently. "I thought you were only going to say it once."

He sighed, struggling to keep his temper. What *was* it about this pint-size woman that brought all of his emotions out in the open? He hardly ever lost his temper, hardly ever *had* a temper to lose. She had made it part of his everyday life. "I don't have time to play games. They're going to need every pair of hands they can get."

He wasn't sure just how many men were on the roster now. The number of volunteers changed from week to week. He, Luc and Shayne were practically the only steady members on the volunteer force.

"My point exactly. I'm not coming to watch. I'm coming to help." Marta looked at him, trying to appeal to his common sense. She had never fit into the "good little woman" mold and never would. "There has to be something I can do to free up someone bigger and stronger to do the things that require more strength."

His foot on the brake, he disengaged the hand control. "You are the damnedest, most stubborn woman…"

"Yes, I am," she agreed wholeheartedly, turning forward. "Now drive."

He shifted the car into drive, and it roared to life. Ike could still make out the last car that had left the field. Picking his way across the snow as quickly as he could, he made a beeline for it.

He spared Marta a glance. She was sitting ramrod

straight beside him, staring into the night as if searching for the fire. The woman was irritating as hell, but she was also magnificent.

He had to know. "What is this burning desire, if you'll pardon the pun, that you have to come along?"

Marta's first instinct was to make up some flippant excuse. But he was bringing her, and maybe she owed him an explanation. Or maybe saying it aloud would take the heavy weight that had suddenly materialized off her chest. It had been a long time since she had thought of it.

"When I was ten years old, the family I was staying with, the Andersons—Edith and John—had their house burn down. It happened in the middle of the night."

She lowered her voice as the memory became more vivid. "I can remember the terror of waking up and seeing flames shooting up all around the room I slept in." It had been a spare bedroom that had been turned into a den and then turned back into a bedroom again when she had come to stay with them. "If it hadn't been for that fireman finding me, I wouldn't be here today."

He'd come out of nowhere—a tall, strapping man dressed all in yellow and black, and she'd thought he was some sort of monster, coming out of the fire to get her. Until she'd seen his eyes. She'd always remember those eyes. Dark brown and kind. The moment she looked into them, she knew he was going to save her.

Ike reached for her hand, covering it. "Remind me to send him a thank-you note."

Marta ignored the comment, thinking it was only a line Ike would have said to anyone. If he sounded sincere when he said it to her, well, that was probably nothing more than part of his well-honed act.

She refused to get caught up in this man's charm any more than she already was. Doggedly, she continued with her story, getting to the heart of it. "I also remember what it felt like, standing out on the lawn, wearing the jacket he'd draped over me. Watching everything those people had burn up. Everything I had, too." Her voice turned wistful. "My favorite toy went up in that blaze."

She hadn't thought about that in years, Marta realized.

"What was it?" Ike asked when she stopped abruptly.

Marta closed her eyes for a second, seeing the stuffed animal in her mind's eye. She couldn't remember who had given it to her, only that she'd always had it. Until the night of the fire.

She laughed softly. "A champagne-colored teddy bear with curly hair. Glen," she recalled. "I called it Glen. I have no idea why. It was pretty ratty by that time." She meant to sound dismissive, but didn't quite carry it off. "I cried for days after that—when no one was around to see."

She'd been proud, even at ten, Ike thought. At what age did a personality take shape? Hers had probably formed a great deal faster than most.

"Keeping a stiff upper lip's pretty important to you, isn't it?"

Marta shrugged, realizing she'd said too much already. He had a way of bringing it out of her. She turned away from him and stared straight ahead. "I like my privacy."

"Sometimes," he told her quietly, "privacy can be lonelier than Hades."

She didn't know whether he was being cryptic, or literal. In either case, she didn't want to continue talking about her past. Looking out her window, she still couldn't see anything. Had someone played a prank on everyone? "Do you know what's burning?"

Yes, he knew. It was Jean Luc who'd sounded the alarm and then called Shayne on his cell phone. Returning to the Salty to tend bar, Luc had seen the fire through the window. "It's the general store."

Ike set his mouth grimly. The general store was their equivalent of "the mall." Without it, they were going to have to do without, or travel into Anchorage. Unless the roads suddenly cleared on their own, the only access anyone had to the city was Shayne, now that Sydney had been officially grounded. It made life difficult for everyone.

"A lot of people might have to tighten their belts for a stretch, unless we're lucky enough to keep the damage to a minimum."

He took this personally, Marta thought. Someone else might look for a way to capitalize on the situation. She knew enough people like that. Had loved someone like that. Or thought she had, she amended.

Now she wasn't so sure.

As soon as she saw the fire, it took center stage, eradicating any other thoughts. Red and yellow flames were reaching out, trying to grasp the sky, even as they licked at the source of their existence.

She hadn't expected the terror to return, but it had. The terror that had taken hold of her that night so long ago. She struggled to wrench herself from its control and lock it away. She hadn't come along to be a burden, but to help.

The lone truck the community possessed, purchased through a pooling of funds, was already in place before the general store. Luc, his hastily donned yellow coat flapping in the wind as he moved, was hurrying to attach the hose to the hydrant. One of the men she remembered seeing at the Salty—a man she'd heard referred to as Clancy—was dispensing protective uniforms as if he were dealing out cards from a giant deck.

"One size fits all?" she asked Ike as she quickly got out of the Jeep.

"Seemed the way to go." Hurrying to secure his uniform, Ike suddenly stopped dead before he reached Clancy. A thought had occurred to him with the suddenness of a summer shower. "You're not going in."

It wasn't a question, it was an order. And because it was, Marta bristled at it, ignoring the protective underpinnings of his instruction. He wasn't being protective, she told herself, he was just worried she'd get in the way.

Marta glared at him over his presumption. Just because they'd made love didn't give him the right to order her around. "I said I wanted to help, not argue. I'll be where I can be the most use."

Ike had no idea what that meant in Marta terms. Exasperated, he turned to Shayne. "Here, you do something with her. She's not going to listen to me."

Already decked out in firefighting gear, Shayne looked surprised to see her. "I thought you were going home with Sydney?"

"Change of plans," was all she said. "What can I do to help?"

Hustling her out of the way of the two volunteers manning the hose, Shayne brought her to where Clancy was dragging out more gear.

"You take over for Clancy. Clancy, tell her what to do and then come find me."

If Clancy was confused by the switch, he gave no indication. There was no time to move slowly or ponder anything. They'd practiced this periodically. Every man knew that every second counted. The general store was close enough to other buildings that the fire would ignite them if the wind picked up even slightly. The entire town could be wiped out in a matter of hours.

Standing near the truck, Marta could feel the searing heat. The blaze, hypnotic and evil, had already consumed a third of the building, its appetite driving it on to destroy the rest. She tore her eyes away, refusing to look for Ike in the crowd. She wouldn't be of any use if she let worry paralyze her.

She looked up at Clancy on the back of the truck. He'd been throwing down the gear that was stashed beneath the seats. Grasping the side rails, she climbed up onto the truck.

"Go," she ordered Clancy. "I can do this."

Grabbing a set of gear for himself, he jumped off the truck and was gone before the words were completely out of her mouth.

It took them over an hour—twelve men working frantically, pitting themselves against a single destructive force, bent on bringing its reign of terror to an abrupt end.

At one point, sparks from the blaze had landed on the roof of the Salty. From her vantage point, Marta had a clear view of the other building. It took her only a second to realize that she was the only one who saw where the sparks had landed, or even that they'd found a target. Appalled, she scanned the area for Ike. Her heart instantly leapt into her throat as she saw him emerging from the burning building, smoke billowing out from behind him as he carried the Kelloggs' aging dog to safety.

He'd risked his life for a dog. Her heart swelled.

"Ike!"

He saw her then, soot streaked across her face, her hair the color of the flames they were trying to beat back. For a second, Ike thought she'd come running to him because she'd been afraid for his life. But then he saw that she was pointing at something.

He looked in the direction she indicated.

Damn!

Rushing past her, he alerted the volunteers in charge of the hose of this newest threat. They directed the water to the Salty's roof before it, too, fell victim to the fire. Because she'd alerted them in time, the threat was averted quickly enough.

Ike's eyes met hers. He hoped she understood. He had no time to say anything to her, to voice his gratitude.

The general store was still burning.

Exhausted, Shayne made the rounds in the bar where the men had gathered after putting out the fire. He was checking the men out for any smoke inhalation or injuries sustained during the fire. A couple of the men had singed hair, and one had swallowed more than his share of smoke. But he was all right. And, more importantly, Tate and Shirley Kellogg, who lived above the store, had been spared along with Isaiah, the dog Ike had carried out after the couple had been rescued. They'd been lucky.

"How about you?" Shayne asked Marta, stopping at her table. "Are you all right?"

She nodded, surprised at how drained she felt. She hadn't actually fought the fire, yet it had taken its toll on her, just being close. With a deep sigh, she dragged her hand through her hair.

"I'm fine."

He checked her out anyway, then turned just as Ike approached with a mug of ale in each hand. "I'll get yours in a minute," he promised Shayne, nodding at the mugs.

"None for me," Shayne told him. "I just want you to sit down so I can check you out."

Ike smiled at Marta. She'd been terrific tonight. As fearless as they came. He felt something warm stir within him. The lady really was something. "I'd rather have your houseguest check me out."

"That's between you and her to settle. Open your mouth," Shayne instructed, a fresh tongue depressor in his hand.

Sighing, Ike complied. When Shayne was finished, Ike nodded toward another table. "Go play doctor with someone else. I've business to attend to."

As Shayne went to examine the men at the next table, Ike sank down into the chair opposite Marta. "Had enough excitement for one day?"

Marta pulled the mug over to her, clasping it in both hands. She took a long swallow before answering, not trusting the condition of her throat to do anything but croak a reply. It was as dry as any of the burned ruins left in the fire's wake. "I'd say yes, more than enough, thank you."

He leaned over. When he reached for her face,

Marta drew her head away, a question in her eyes. "You've got some soot on your chin."

Before she could remedy the situation herself, Ike took her chin in his hand. Using his thumb, he rubbed away the long streak. For the life of him, he couldn't explain why that aroused him, but it did. It seemed that everything about her aroused him. She was like whiskey, taken straight on an empty stomach. She made his head spin.

He didn't sit back right away. "I don't know how to thank you."

Marta struggled to get her bearings. She'd felt calmer during the fire than she did now. She feigned interest in her drink. "For what?"

Ike was surprised she had to ask, but then, they'd all been through a great deal tonight. And he would have bet any amount of money that this was all new to her.

"If you hadn't seen those sparks land on the roof, there's no telling how much damage the Salty would have sustained. We were all so involved with the general store, my saloon could easily have burned down."

Marta didn't want him thanking her for that. She felt restless, and unsure what it was she wanted from him. Other than peace. "I just saw it first." She took another long sip. "Someone had to."

He'd made her uncomfortable again, he realized. Why? "You don't take compliments very well, do you?"

Marta looked away. Maybe it was time they were

leaving. But when she looked for Shayne, he was busy talking to someone at the bar. So much for a quick getaway. ''I don't know what you're talking about.''

He placed his hand over hers, bringing her attention back to him. ''Yes, you do. Every time I try to say something nice to you, you practically slam it back at me, like a tennis ball you're determined to lob over the net. You're afraid that if you don't, you might lose the championship.''

Marta opened her mouth to deny it, but she discovered that she just didn't have the strength. Instead, she lifted her shoulder in a half shrug. ''Maybe I just don't trust compliments.'' A defiant look entered her eyes. ''They're usually just empty words, anyway.''

Ike felt himself bristling. She was lumping him in with others she'd known. ''You're never going to be able to enjoy yourself and what life has to offer if you don't put yesterday behind you.''

They'd made love today, not yesterday. What was he talking about? Marta wondered. ''Yesterday?''

''Your yesterday,'' he clarified. ''All your yesterdays.'' Ike closed his hand over hers. She was feisty as all hell, and yet he couldn't get over the impression that she was really a vulnerable woman who needed someone to lean on. She'd probably have his head if she could read his thoughts. ''Life can only go forward if you do.''

She pulled her hand away, dropping it in her lap.

"I'm moving ahead just fine, thank you. You don't have to worry about me."

"Maybe I don't have to." A smile played on his lips as he tucked a stray hair behind her ear. "Doesn't mean I won't. You're quite a woman, Marta Jensen, no matter how much you want me to think you're not."

She looked away. You'd think, after everything she'd been through tonight, that her stomach wouldn't turn to gelatin just because he'd skimmed his fingers along her face. "Doesn't matter to me what you think."

He rose to his feet, and Marta thought she'd finally managed to chase him away. It was what she wanted, she told herself.

And yet...

Instead of leaving her table, Ike raised his mug and called for everyone's attention.

"I'd like to propose a toast." He looked down at her and grinned when he saw the uncertainty in her eyes. "To Marta Jensen. If it wasn't for this little darlin', we'd all be doing our drinking in the snow right now—if we even had anything to drink."

That drew a wave of groans and protests from the men as they contemplated life without a retreat. Almost in unison, they all raised their mugs and shouted, "To Marta Jensen, savior of the Salty Saloon."

Laughing, feeling perhaps a little more of the beer than she'd intended, Marta raised her mug to toast the men who were toasting her. In the spirit of the moment, she raised the mug to her lips.

The next thing she knew, she was engulfed by the men. Someone began singing a chorus of "For She's a Jolly Good Fellow." Within seconds, everyone was singing along. Two men closest to her suddenly hoisted her onto their shoulders. The men were not of equal height, and she found herself listing.

Laughing, clutching their shoulders, Marta tried to steady herself. The men who had been so tired only moments ago carried her around the bar and continued singing, mostly off-key. They came to an abrupt stop right before the bar, as if they hadn't realized it was there. Caught off guard, Marta began slipping forward in an ignoble dismount. She would have fallen had Ike not been there to catch her. And bring her to a jarring halt.

Her body slid along the length of his until her feet reached the ground.

Urgent messages telegraphed themselves all up and down her nerve endings, begging for a repeat of the morning they had shared.

She was going to have to do something about this, she told herself. And soon, if she was going to maintain her dignity, let alone her sanity.

Dignity faded quickly when she saw the look in Ike's eyes.

Chapter Fourteen

Like smoke filling her lungs, eating away at her air supply, Marta caught her breath as the realization came. Why hadn't she seen it before?

Why hadn't she realized that looking into Ike's eyes was exactly like looking into the eyes of that fireman who had saved her life so long ago?

Because it wasn't the same, her mind insisted. Yes, the color was the same, and yes, there might have been that same warm glint to them that had once created the feeling within her that she was safe, that no harm would come to her. But it wasn't the same, not really. One was true; the other, just a distorted childhood memory. An illusion, nothing more.

But looking into Ike's eyes, she couldn't seem to shake the feeling.

And then Shayne was behind her, gently placing a hand on her shoulder and intruding on the moment. And dissolving the last remnants of the illusion.

"Everyone seems to be okay, so I think I'll be heading home," he said. "You want to come along and pick up Celine, or would you rather we kept her for the night?"

The thought of another sleepless night stacked on top of the day he'd just had sapped the last of Ike's energy. He flashed a grateful smile at the suggestion. "If Sydney doesn't mind..."

"You know Sydney, she never minds when it comes to kids." Shayne looked at Marta. "Ready?"

"Ready." She turned away from Ike, feeling as if she'd just been saved from making a huge mistake.

And very possibly, from experiencing another delicious interlude.

But that, she reminded herself as she sat next to Shayne on the way home a few minutes later, was all it was, even at its best. Just an interlude. And wonderful though the lovemaking had been, she needed no more interludes in her life. What she craved now, what she'd always craved, was something permanent. That just wasn't in the cards, not here with Ike. There was no reason to invest her emotions, or her heart.

No reason at all.

Except maybe for a pair of brown eyes that saw

into her soul, and a mouth that made her burn when it touched hers.

Ike sat back on his heels, watching. Waiting for the fire he was coaxing to life in the fireplace to take hold. There was a chill in the air that the electricity—now that it was finally turned on—couldn't manage to vanquish. Crackling sounds accompanied the struggle. He breathed a sigh of satisfaction as the small flames began to multiply, growing stronger.

Rising, he dusted off his hands on his jeans and turned around to look at Marta.

She was sitting, rocking Celine. Rocking her in the very same rocking chair where his mother had once sat, rocking Junie. Warm feelings began to cascade through him, and he smiled to himself. It wasn't in him to dwell on the sadness, only the good times.

Like now.

This was the first time he and Marta had been alone since he'd made love with her last week.

Last week? It felt more like an eternity ago. And it was, if he measured it in longing. In nights spent imagining her beside him.

She was probably the only woman on earth who could reduce him to the state of an awkward teen. Words didn't seem to come easily to him around her.

Just feelings.

Like the ones he was having now. Strange, foreign feelings. Feelings, he thought, that he would have attributed to people like Shayne. But not to him.

And yet, here he was, having them. And not knowing what the hell to do about them, or even *if* he wanted to do anything about them.

"This wasn't exactly a typical week, you know," Ike said, approaching her. She looked at him quizzically, as if she hadn't expected him to talk. "Fires usually don't break out, and we don't usually have marathon house-raising sessions, fixing up one place, much less two." The moment his house had been set to rights, the town had turned its attention to clearing away the debris that had once been the walls and ground floor of the general store, and rebuilding it.

"And babies." He crouched until he was down to Celine's level. Ever so gently, he glided his hand over her soft hair. She stirred in Marta's arms. And in his heart. "Babies don't usually drop out of the sky into my lap."

It was the only way he could say it, the only way he could divorce himself from the pain that having Celine in his life represented. Because if she weren't here, it would mean that Junie still would be somewhere.

Resting his hands on the arm of the rocker, Ike looked up at Marta. She could feel her stomach tightening. It had to stop, Marta told herself sternly.

It didn't.

"Well, maybe not dropping out of the sky," she

allowed, trying very hard to sound disinterested, detached. "But I would have thought there'd be at least a handful floating around somewhere with your features stamped on their faces."

Ike caught himself thinking how perfect her face seemed. How tempting her mouth was. Damn, but he wanted her. He released the rocker arm, afraid he'd grip it just a little too hard.

"No, no small tribe with LeBlanc blood in their veins." He rose to his feet. "I would have known, and I would have taken full responsibility."

"Then that would make you a very exceptional man."

Moving very carefully, she rose with Celine in her arms. She crossed to the small room that had been converted into a nursery and placed the baby into the crib that she had helped Ike put together just yesterday. It had been in the attic, dismantled because of a lack of space. There was other furniture in the room as well. A bureau and a bassinet had arrived in a cargo plane piloted by Jeb Kellogg. A former resident of Hades, Jeb had recently moved on to Anchorage. Now he made occasional runs for the various stores in the city to deliver items purchased by people living in the far corners of the region that were too large to be brought back in private Cessnas. Jeb had made his drop, then gone to see his family for an extended visit. Learning of their close call had shaken him.

It had taken the better part of yesterday to put everything together and at any given time, there had been three of them at it. Shayne and Sydney had come by, as well as Jean Luc and a few of Ike's other friends.

Ike stood in the doorway now of the baby's room, his arms crossed before him, watching Marta. Wondering what it would be like if he were watching his wife cover their baby.

The thought caught him by surprise.

Marta could feel him watching her. Could feel his eyes sweeping along her body. Could feel herself growing warm. It was time to leave. *Quickly.*

She walked past him, not sparing Ike even a glance. "I guess I'd better be getting back."

It didn't surprise Marta that he followed her. Or that he stopped her, his hand on her arm. "Do you have to go so soon?"

She had an excuse all ready. An escape plan all mapped out. "I'm leaving the day after tomorrow, and so far I've spent more time with you and Celine than I have with the person I came to see. Sydney," she added in case he was going to say something flippant and somehow turn the focus back on himself.

As if every part of her wasn't already focused on him.

He moved his hands from her arms to her shoulders. His thumbs teased the hoops at her ears, sending them swaying in tandem. "Has it been that hard on you, being here with us?"

"No." Her eyes on his, she caught the hoops and

stilled them. "Although I have to admit I think you're not as inept as you pretend."

A small, seductive smile crept over his lips and under her skin, making her so achingly aware of him. Of how close he was standing to her.

"That depends on what you're referring to. If you mean caring for Celine, then you'd be surprised at how inept I can be." Very slowly, still talking, still looking into her eyes, Ike ran his fingertip along her chin. He felt her shiver forming before she stifled it. "If you mean something else—" his smile went deep into her soul "—then I think this is where I should be taking offense."

Her eyes glinted. "Relax, I wasn't talking about your manhood."

He couldn't remember ever wanting a woman this much. Or *enjoying* wanting a woman this much. "Why talk about it when you could be doing something about it?" Visions of how she'd been with him that afternoon began to play through his mind, wreaking havoc over his restraint. He ran the back of his hand along her cheek. "Or with it."

Marta felt her eyes begin to drift shut, felt everything else begin to wake up. She could feel the struggle within her heightening, could feel the final outcome forming.

She'd promised herself this wasn't going to happen again. So far, she'd been able to maintain at least some distance between them since the afternoon on which he'd initiated her into a whole new world of lovemaking. Even when they'd put the baby furniture together, there had always been someone around. She'd made sure of that, asking Sydney to come and help, and to spread the word that they needed skilled input.

But she'd spread no such word today. There was nothing left to put together, except perhaps the crumbling fences she'd had up around her heart. They were in jeopardy of disintegrating completely, leaving her exposed.

She wished Sydney were here. Or she were there.

She wished she didn't want him as much as she did.

Marta tried to clear her throat. Dust would have found it too dry to remain. She tried to muster as much conviction as she could. "I really think I should go."

Ike wasn't about to strong-arm Marta into staying, even though he wanted her to more than he thought was humanly possible. "Okay, but I have something for you before you go."

She would have thought he would put up a little more of a fight to get her to stay. It only went to show how wrong she could be about a man. About men in general.

Wondering if he thought of himself as the supreme gift, she raised a skeptical brow at his wording. "Oh?"

Ike caught her drift immediately and laughed. "No, not that. You already made it pretty clear that you weren't interested." There was more than a shade of regret in his voice. "Wait here."

Curious now, she felt herself growing impatient as she waited for him to return. If he wasn't euphemistically referring to himself, she couldn't imagine what—

Her eyes widened when she saw what he had in his hands. Marta's hands flew up to her lips. "Oh, my God."

The instant she saw the silly, champagne-colored stuffed animal, her eyes welled up so quickly that they threatened to overflow, just the way her heart did a moment later.

"I thought you might like to have this." He handed it to her.

"Glen." The bear looked just like the one she'd lost, except that he was a lot less worn. She blinked back the tears even as she combed her fingers through the silky fur. Memories crowded into her head. She raised her eyes, looking at Ike. He probably thought she was an idiot, behaving this way. "Where did you get it?"

Ike couldn't remember ever feeling this pleased giving a gift before. "Mayfield's department store."

Jeb had delivered the toy to him a few minutes before Marta had arrived this morning. He'd paid the man twice the going rate for the pickup. But then, it was a very special bear. One that had taken Ike the better part of a week to locate. The fur was straight, not curly the way she'd described. "It's probably not exactly like the one you lost, but this was as close as I could find."

"How did you—?"

He grinned. "We do have phones that work here. I called around with a description. I never realized how many different toy stores there are in Anchorage and Fairbanks." That's why it had taken him this long to find the bear. Feeling just the slightest bit awkward in the face of her tears, he pretended to fiddle with the red bow around the bear's neck, adjusting it. "I thought maybe, when you looked at it, you'd remember Celine." His eyes met hers. "And me."

"Oh, I'll remember you, all right."

He heard the tears in her voice, saw a couple spill out and slide down her cheeks. Had he been wrong? Did the bear bring back painful memories for her? "I didn't give that to you to make you cry."

Marta pressed her lips together, calling herself an idiot. She was supposed to be made of tougher stuff than this. She tightened her arms around the teddy bear, pressing it to her chest. "I know. I love it."

He pretended to eye the stuffed animal. "Right now, I think I'm a little envious of that bear, being where it is."

"Wait a second." Acting on impulse, Marta placed the bear on the sofa and turned to hug Ike.

He held up a hand, stopping her. Picking up the bear, he turned it around so that it faced the sofa. Ike winked at her. "Wouldn't want him getting an education before his time."

Unable to help herself, Marta laughed. The laughter felt good. Almost as good as his arms felt around her. She had slipped into them easily. Looking up, she shook her head, mystified.

"I don't know what to make of you." He kept doing things that were at odds with the niche she'd mentally placed him in. He refused to stay put.

He combed his fingers through her hair, sweeping it away from her face. "Do you have to try?"

"Yes," she answered honestly. Because he'd been kind to her, more than kind, she wanted him to understand. "Being naive has hurt me a great deal."

Unable to resist, Ike brushed a soft kiss against her lips. The thrill went deep, an arrow shot into the center of his core.

"You weren't naive, Marta, you were trusting, with a trusting heart. And you wanted to be loved." All one kiss did was make him want another. He had a feeling there was no end to that feeling. But he'd enjoy conducting his own experiment to find out. "Nothing wrong with that. We all want to be loved in our own way."

"And yours would be to be loved by as many women as possible?" There was humor sparkling in her eyes as she asked.

He inclined his head. "There are a great many definitions of love." Very slowly, he anointed her mouth with his own, taking care not to be too rough, not to frighten her away.

"No, there aren't," she whispered against his mouth, a moan echoing in her veins. "There's only love, or the absence of it."

They were talking too much. Not loving enough. And he wanted to. He wanted to love every inch of her, for as long as possible. And even a little longer than that.

Passing his hands slowly along the length of her, Ike filled his hands with her, worshipping what he touched with every movement he made.

He wanted to enjoy her, to enjoy every inch, every curve, every beat of her heart. But a sense of urgency filled him, as if he knew he had to outrun not only time but a host of other demons before they took hold of both of them: the ghost of a lover not yet gone from her memory, and love too long elusive.

He stood back, looking at her, his hands linked with hers. Though he'd undressed her with his eyes, and in his mind, he'd yet to take a single garment off her. It didn't matter. Not in the way he saw her.

"You are so beautiful."

Marta wasn't going to let the words get to her, wasn't going to allow her head to be turned to the point that she couldn't find her way out of this heated maze. Even though she knew she was going to make love with him, she couldn't lose sight of the end. Or of the fact that this was just exquisite physical love, and nothing more. Not for him.

And so it couldn't be for her.

"What I am," she whispered as he pressed his lips to her throat, driving her crazy, "is here."

His words hummed along her skin. His breath

drove her crazy. "And I've never been so grateful for anything in my life, darlin'."

Darlin'. The neutral term. But she didn't care. There was so little time left, and in the moments she had, she wanted to be his. His "darlin'." Wanted to be all things to him so that, despite all the women who had been in his life and all the women who were to come, the moments he shared with her would stand out for him.

Feeling like a tigress prowling the terrain one last time before she was returned to her cage, Marta allowed herself to break free of restraints. Allowed herself to stop thinking of the moment as something that would soon vanish. Instead, it became something for her to live within. To live for the moment because there was only now.

Only him.

She took Ike's breath away. One moment, her mouth was upturned to his, her sighs throbbing in his brain, the next, he felt her hands racing along his body, pulling off his shirt, raking over his hips.

Stunned, he caught her hands, looking at her. "Marta?"

She twisted out of his hold. "Don't talk. Just make love with me," she breathed.

"Yes, ma'am." He took control. Or tried to. What resulted was an unspoken competition in which each tried to pleasure and outdo the other by raising that pleasure to a new high.

They both lost.

They both won.

He'd never felt like this, never felt as if he couldn't catch his breath, as if it was a struggle to keep his wits about him. When she strained against him, he could barely hold himself in check. The desire to plunge himself into her, to feel her seal herself around him, accepting this most intimate of unions, almost overwhelmed him.

It was like being presented with a feast and wanting to sample everything at once, to eat and yet remain hungry enough to eat more. And he wanted more, so much more of her.

His heart quickened at the same time as his loins did, when she urgently pressed herself against him. When he heard her moan as his hands covered her buttocks, pressing her even closer. So close that he thought he would absorb her. Be absorbed by her.

He wanted to conquer this feeling, to rise above it and be able to look down on it from a safe perch, the way he'd always been able to before.

But there was no conquering, there was only being conquered. And he couldn't rise above it. Instead, he was engulfed by it and in it. Engulfed by it and by her. Engulfed in the magic her slightest sigh created. Her slightest movement.

If this was insanity—and he suspected that it had to be—it was a wonderful insanity. He hoped he'd never recover.

Pinning her to the floor, he kissed her over and over again, tracing his lips along her throat, her breasts, the quivering rise and fall of her belly. And quested ever farther.

He heard her stifle a scream and knew that he had brought her up and over the first crest. But there were more crests to meet, more peaks to conquer. More to give her.

Marta thought she'd bitten through her lip that time, stopping herself at the last minute from shouting out loud and waking up the baby. And quite possibly the whole town.

Blindly, she felt for his shoulders, her fingers digging into his muscles. With the last bit of clarity left to her, she pressed her hands to his flesh, urging him back up to face her. To take her one last time and to make the journey with her.

His heart pounding, he drew the length of his body over hers. His body quickening, hardening at the tantalizing contact. Perspiration mingled and sealed as he entered her and took her to somewhere they had already been.

Somewhere new.

"I love you."

Chapter Fifteen

Marta's eyes sprang open.

She wasn't sure if she'd heard him, or if the words were just echoing in her head—shadows of what existed in her heart, so tightly under wraps.

Her heart still beating erratically from the wild ride they had just taken each other on, she turned her head toward him.

The words took Ike aback, even though they were his. They had just slipped out on a wave of emotion, as if they had wills of their own. He smiled to himself, feeling a little shaken. Raising himself up on his elbows, Ike framed Marta's face and looked at her. What was she thinking? She hadn't said anything to him in return.

Was he alone in his feelings? He didn't think so,

but he couldn't tell for sure. Couldn't really tell what she was feeling because he wasn't completely certain what it was that *he* was feeling. If pressed right now, he couldn't say whether it was just the moment, or the thought of her leaving that had prompted him to say what he had.

Or whether it was simply the woman.

The woman who had created the feeling within him and brought the words to his lips. Ever since he'd first kissed her in the airport, she had stirred him up something fierce, leaving him a man without a compass, trying to find his way in the wilderness.

The silence was stretching out to unbearable lengths. "You know, I never said that to another woman before. Not where it meant something."

Was he trying to tell her something, or just rescind the words themselves? Marta wondered. "But you said it when it didn't mean anything?" She struggled not to cling to the words, not to believe them. Because once she did, once she pretended that he meant them, even for a tiny space of time, then discovering otherwise would hurt twice as much. Maybe even more. Was there anything worse than wanting love and being cheated of it? She doubted it.

But the sound of the three little words was, oh, so seductive.

It wasn't jealousy in her eyes. Ike knew what jealousy looked like, knew the signs. She wasn't jealous of the women who had come before.

"No, I've said it to my mother, to Junie." Two women who had been so important to his life. And now there was a new woman, a smaller version who needed him. He would always be there for her, to give Celine whatever it was she needed. But he also had needs of his own. Needs that Marta had made him aware of.

If the two had been the only ones to hear the words from him, Marta could have accepted that. But she knew that a man like Ike could no more refrain from telling women what they wanted to hear than he could stop breathing. It was just part of his nature to be accommodating, to be charming.

"And to every other female within earshot," she guessed.

Ike could feel her stiffening, withdrawing. He blocked her retreat, at least physically, bracketing her head between his hands so that she couldn't turn away from him. "No, not where I meant the words. Do you have to leave?" It wasn't a question, it was an entreaty. He didn't think she realized how much of himself he was risking by asking.

Marta closed her eyes, wishing her body didn't want him so. That she didn't ache to believe the words that probably even now were being forgotten. "Not for a few hours."

She was being evasive, Ike thought. Why? Why was she drawing away from him? "I meant Hades—do you have to leave Hades so soon? You just got here."

It felt as if Marta had just set foot in Hades, and yet it felt as if she'd been here far longer than the two weeks that her round-trip ticket boasted. Pitching in to help in the fire, being part of the reconstruction that came in the aftermath, she felt more at home here than she ever had anywhere else.

But she wasn't Sydney. She couldn't just pull up stakes and replant herself so far away from everything that was now familiar. She'd been uprooted so many times before. She just didn't have it in her to do it again. She had a life back in Omaha. A job, responsibilities. People who depended on her.

And an empty apartment.

She ran her tongue along her lips, moistening them. The spark she saw entering Ike's eyes almost made her forget what she was going to say. "I'll be back in the summer. And maybe even during spring break if I can manage it." That was coming up in April. It would only be for a week, but at least it would be something. "The baby will be here by then, and Sydney'll welcome the extra help."

Her breasts rose and fell with each breath she took, moving so invitingly against Ike's chest. The urge to take her again, to make love with her until both their bodies and minds were numb was appealing. But he couldn't use that as a tool, no matter how tempting it was. It wouldn't be fair to either of them.

He wanted her to be honest with him.

He wanted her to remain with him. Because of him. Somewhere, he thought, a man named Murphy was laughing because his law was being invoked. All the women who had been through his life, who would willingly have remained—and he wanted the one who was resisting.

"So you'll be coming back because of Sydney?"

Was that hurt in his voice? Marta wondered. No, maybe injured vanity, but not hurt. Still, her breath caught in her throat as she looked up at him. Wanting him despite everything. "Should there be another reason?"

Something sharp tore within Ike, ravaging his pride. "Well, hell, I guess you've got a lot of men telling you they love you, then. What I just said probably just washed off your back."

Did he think she was insensitive? Didn't he know how much she ached to hear the words? To hear the words spoken with genuine feeling, instead of just popping out at the spur of the moment? "I don't take the words 'I love you' lightly."

His eyes held hers. And darkened. "I don't say them lightly."

Marta couldn't allow herself to believe him. She couldn't be hurt again. Because she knew that what she felt for Ike was so much more than it ever was for Alex. And that put her at greater risk than ever before. "I have to go."

For a moment, just a moment, Ike thought of refusing. Of keeping her here until she admitted to her feelings. But maybe he was just making it all up in his head. Maybe he wanted her to love him so much that he was reading things into every word she said, every look she spared him.

Sighing, Ike rolled off her, allowing Marta to get up. But he didn't avert his eyes as she scrambled to her feet. Instead, he watched her, memorizing every movement. Angry he still wanted her.

Dead, he'd probably still want her, he thought.

Completely unselfconscious as to his naked state, he propped up his head on his palm. If she hurried any faster into her clothes, her hands would get tangled. "You know, maybe it's the weather, or maybe it's the pace out here. Or maybe I'm just slow. But I don't understand why you're acting as if you suddenly realized I have the plague."

She jammed her arms through her sweater, then pulled it up over her head. She wished she could just close her eyes and vanish, instead of enduring this awkward interlude as she got dressed.

"You don't have the plague, you have a mouth dipped in honey. According to Sydney, you can turn any woman's head, and I don't doubt it." She ran her hands through her hair, knowing she had to look like hell. "You're good-looking, you know how to say just the right words. One look from you and a woman's knees turn to mush. And heaven knows you've turned lovemaking into an art form."

So far, she hadn't said anything that gave him a clue as to why she was running from him. "There's a 'but' coming here, isn't there?"

She nodded, the words sticking in her throat as she forced them out. "But I'm not about to sell my heart for a one-night stand, or even a two-night stand."

Was that what she thought of him? After he'd gone out of his way to show her otherwise?

He struggled to maintain the easygoing facade that had once been his natural bent. "I wasn't asking you for your heart," he lied. "I was just telling you how I felt. If that bothers you, then I'm sorry, but there's no need to run off half-cocked, or half dressed.''

His eyes slid very slowly down her lower torso. Marta looked down and her cheeks heated instantly. In her hurry to get dressed, she'd somehow managed to neglect to put on her jeans. Embarrassed, she grabbed them from the floor and yanked them on.

Ike didn't want her leaving this way. Getting to his feet, he stopped only long enough to put his own jeans on.

''Look, maybe I shouldn't have said anything.'' It was as close as he could bring himself to apologizing for saying something that he felt. ''It just seemed like the right thing to say at the time.'' He caught her hand, forcing her to look at him. ''Marta, I've never felt like this before.''

Another reason for his words began to materialize in her mind. It made far more sense than his loving her. ''You've never been in a position like this before.''

Ike realized that his grip was tightening, and he loosened his fingers around her wrist. But he still held on. ''Meaning what?''

Why hadn't she realized this before? Marta had walked in on Shayne and Ike talking about this very thing last week. A woman who could fill three capacities. Ike had called it 'killing three birds with one stone.' It made so much sense. She'd practically embraced the role as caretaker. ''Meaning you suddenly have a child to raise. Maybe you think it would be nice to share the burden.''

"Responsibility," he corrected tersely. "Celine's not a burden." He still didn't see where she was going with this, or why she was suddenly so upset. He hadn't done anything but love her. "And maybe I do think it would be nice to share raising her with someone. So what?"

Did he think she was blind? Or just too enamored to see? "So what you're really looking for is someone to warm your bed at night and to take care of Celine during the day."

Ike's eyes narrowed. She made it sound like a business deal. Worse, she made him sound like a man he'd loathe. A man who used people. Wounded that she'd think so little of him, and annoyed with himself for caring, he struggled to keep from shouting at her.

"What I'd be looking for—if I were looking— is a woman who doesn't blow hot and cold in the space of one rotation of the minute hand."

Why she suddenly felt like crying was beyond her, but Marta knew she had to get out before she made an even greater fool of herself. She grabbed her parka. "Maybe it's the company I keep—ever stop to think of that?"

She shoved her arms through the sleeves, then, fumbling with the parka's zipper, she stormed out, slamming the door.

He stared at the closed door. What the hell had just happened here? Ike dragged his hand through his hair, angry and mystified at the same time. He'd just told her he loved her. That wasn't supposed to have made everything blow up in his face. Why had it?

He saw the bear on the sofa, the one he'd gotten for her. She'd left it behind. Just like she'd left him.

For two cents, he'd wring her neck for turning him inside out like this. For less than that, he'd drag her back and force her to—

To what? To make love with him again? That wasn't his style.

Maybe she didn't love him. Maybe she had been just dallying with him, the way she claimed he did with other women.

Maybe…

Maybe he'd better think about this later. Right now, Celine was crying. At least he could understand her needs.

"I'm coming, darlin', I'm coming. Don't get your diaper all bunched up."

Hand on the nursery doorknob, Ike blew out a frustrated breath. For the first time in his life, he found himself completely stumped by a woman.

Of all the times for that to happen…

"I hate to see you go, Marta."

Marta closed her suitcase, offering Sydney a sad smile. They were in the guest room. Sara and Mac had already said their goodbyes last night and were still in bed, asleep.

Ike hadn't come at all, but then, she hadn't expected him to.

Only wished.

Now there was only this final leave-taking before

she boarded the Cessna with Shayne. She couldn't wait to go.

She wanted to stay, but then, that was just her craziness, that small holdover from her childhood that went hand-in-hand with looking for love. The only love she'd find here was in Sydney's heart.

"I remember saying words to that effect to you a little more than a year ago," said Marta. "Except, I think I substituted 'Sydney' for 'Marta.'" Laughing softly, she gave Sydney a hug. "I'll be back soon, and next time we'll have a real visit. I didn't spend nearly enough time with you," she apologized.

Sydney wouldn't hear it. "You were being Marta. Helpful."

And where did that get her? Miserable and feeling more empty than she had in a very long time. She put the suitcase she'd just packed next to the other two. "No good deed goes unpunished, I guess."

Sydney placed her hand on Marta's shoulder. Something was wrong. Had been now for two days. "You want to tell me about it?"

Marta tried to look puzzled. "About what?"

"About why you came home crying the day before yesterday?"

Having had her suspicions, Sydney had sent Shayne to talk to Ike, but he'd returned saying he'd gotten his head bitten off for his trouble. Whatever had happened between the two, Ike wasn't talking about it. As for Marta, she'd eluded all of Sydney's attempts to get to the heart of the problem. She had no recourse but to be blunt.

It didn't help. Marta pretended to glance around the small room, looking for anything she might have forgotten. In reality she knew the only thing she'd forgotten was to lock up her heart in the first place. "The wind stung my eyes."

Sydney crossed her arms before her. "I don't think I've ever heard him called that before. Ike," she added when Marta didn't say anything.

There was no point in lying, but neither was there any point in elaborating. She wasn't sure she could, except that part of her had secretly hoped he would come looking for her, to talk her out of what she believed in her heart to be true. To convince her that what he'd said to her was true.

"He's probably been called a lot of things you haven't heard firsthand," Marta quipped.

She looked at her watch. It was early, but she wanted to leave in plenty of time to make her flight. Staying here right now would only prolong her anguish. She would go on hoping until she was on the plane heading for home.

Home. The word had never sounded emptier to her.

Because she didn't want to break down in front of Sydney, she changed the subject. "I wish there was another way to get to the airport without bothering Shayne."

"Well, I wish I was the one taking you, but Shayne won't budge on this one." She looked down at her stomach. Only a little while longer, she

promised herself. "And you're not bothering him.
He has to stop at the hospital for new supplies anyway." With a sigh, Sydney hugged her best friend.
"When will you get it through your head that you
don't bother anyone? That having you in our lives
is what makes our lives special?"

Marta made no comment. The fact that Sydney
believed that was good enough for her. She returned
the heartfelt embrace. "I am going to miss you. I
wish I could be here when you have the baby."

"That makes two of us."

Marta pressed her lips together, thinking.
"Maybe I can arrange for a leave of absence—"
There was a substitute teacher she could recom-
mend to cover for her.

"They only do that for family hardship," Sydney
reminded her.

Tucking the smaller suitcase under her arm,
Marta picked up the other two as she saw Shayne
walking toward them. It was time. She looked at
Sydney. "You're the closest thing to a sister I ever
had. I'll do what I can to be here when the time
comes," she promised.

Sydney barely had time to put her sadness away
when she heard the pounding on her front door.
Thinking that Marta had forgotten something, Sydney moved as quickly as she could to the door. She
just managed to step back as Ike barreled into the
house.

"Where is she?"

Now he came. She could have hit him. But one

look at his face banished all thought of lectures.
She'd never quite seen him like this before. "Oh
Ike, you just missed her. She and Shayne left not
more then ten minutes ago. She wanted to get an
early start."

Sydney found herself talking to his back. Ike had
spun on his heel and was hurrying away.

"Good luck!" she shouted after him.

Closing the door again, she shook her head. Men.

Marta couldn't find a place for herself.

She'd turned down Shayne's offer to remain with
her at the airport until she boarded her flight. She
knew his time was precious and that he was in a
hurry to return to Sydney. Besides, she wanted to
be by herself. To somehow make peace with the
sadness that had soaked into her soul like an ink
stain inching its way through fabric. She couldn't
do that and also keep up her end of a conversation
that wasn't registering.

So she'd sent him on his way and had begun to
prowl around the airport terminal, trying to distract
herself—and failing miserably.

All she could think about was Ike.

Because of him, she hadn't had a chance to say
goodbye to Celine. How big would the baby be
when she returned? Babies grew quickly at this age.

Would there be another woman holding her?

Of course there would. There probably was even
now. Alaska might have a female shortage, but Ike
LeBlanc didn't. He had probably forgotten all about
her by now. Why else hadn't he come by the house?

Damn him, anyway.

It felt like an eternity before her flight was finally called. After hearing first boarding announced, Marta turned toward the proper gate and slowly made her way to it, feeling as if each of her legs weighed a ton.

She was going to have to snap out of this, she upbraided herself. It didn't make any sense to feel this way about a man who didn't care.

It didn't change anything.

In a solitary world of her own making, Marta didn't hear a man somewhere behind her excusing himself as he made his way through the crowd heading toward Gate 12. Like a lemming heading toward destruction, she moved with the crowd.

Moved until she suddenly felt herself being scooped up into a pair of strong arms. Her suitcase falling from her hand, Marta bit back a shriek at suddenly losing contact with the floor.

"Excuse me." Ike addressed a man next to him. "Would you mind handing her that suitcase?" He nodded at it. "She just dropped it."

Grinning, the man acted as if nothing out of the ordinary was going on and put the handle into her hand.

"Get a better grip on it," Ike instructed Marta.

Disbelief gave way in Marta to relief, and then slipped into disorientation. She stared at Ike as he proceeded to carry her away from her gate. "What are you doing?" Behind them, people were boarding the plane she was supposed to be on. She and

Ike were moving farther and farther away from it. "Where are you taking me?"

"As far away from the plane as is physically possible," he answered.

"Put me down," she ordered. "I'm going to miss my flight."

"That's the whole idea."

She squirmed, but Ike just held on tighter, strolling with her through the waiting area, garnering a host of interested, amused looks.

Where were the security guards when you needed them? she thought desperately. She didn't want to be dragged back on the emotional roller coaster she'd just jumped from. "This isn't funny, Ike."

He spared her a look from the corner of his eye, then kept his gaze straight ahead. "Didn't mean for it to be, darlin'. You'll know when I'm being funny. Actually, I'd hoped you'd know when I was being serious, but we can work on that." He debated walking right out of the terminal with her, or just finding someplace where they could talk.

"What's this all about?"

"Plummeting business at the Salty, to begin with."

Now she was completely lost. "What?"

"Luc says I'm driving away business, and this is with a trapped clientele." Ike couldn't really say he disagreed with his cousin. He had been pretty surly these last couple of days, trying to sort things out in his head. Trying to tell himself he was better off without her. But a lie was a lie no matter how it was dressed up. He wasn't better off without her, he *needed* her in his life. "I want you to stay. I *need* you to stay. It's not like there's anywhere else to go for a social drink in Hades, so you know I had to be pretty bad."

"What does this have to do with my missing my flight?"

"Everything." He stopped walking and looked into her eyes. "I want you to stay. Please."

The single word cut sharply into her escalating indignation. She was being a fool, Marta told herself. He didn't love her, not really. He just needed someone to care for Celine. She'd heard him say it. If he felt anything for her, he would have come to talk to her after she'd stormed out.

But he was here now.

"Why didn't you come to see me yesterday, or the night before that? If you're serious, why didn't you come after me?"

Ike knew she'd hold that against him, and he couldn't blame her. But he also knew he wouldn't have been able to reach his decision any other way. He didn't like leaping impulsively, and she'd very nearly made him do that. He'd had to stand back and take stock of things. To be sure. For both their sakes.

"I had some soul-searching to do," he told her. "And I found it."

"Found what?"

"My soul. Only problem is, it's determined to board a plane for Omaha."

Words, beautiful words. *Make me believe you,*

Ike. Please make me believe you, Marta pleaded silently. "Put me down, Ike."

Ike looked at her, weighing his options. "Only if you promise not to run."

"I promise."

He believed her. More than that, he knew he could outrun her. Ike set her down slowly, but put his arms around her, just in case. "You know, if you go back on your word, I'll just hunt you down and take you off the next flight. And the one after that."

All Marta had to do was look into his eyes to know he meant it. She let the suitcase slide from her fingers to the floor. "And how many times do you intend to do that?"

"As many times as it takes. Maybe I didn't say it right last time, but I love you. I love you, and I want you to stay. Not for a month, but forever."

"Forever," she repeated. It had such a nice ring to it. She wanted forever. But others in her life had talked about forever, too. "Define forever."

He smiled into her eyes. That was easy. "Until the population of Alaska is equal to that of Southern California."

It suddenly hit her, as another flight was announced over the loudspeaker, that she'd had the only local pilot in Hades—now that Sydney was grounded—and he was now at the hospital. The roads were still impassable. "How did you get here?"

"Jeb Kellogg's still visiting with his family. I bribed him to fly me out here—and don't change the subject." His face became serious. "The only way you're going to get rid of me is by looking me in the eye and telling me that you don't love me."

She tried to look away, but he slowly turned her head back until their eyes met. Marta sighed deeply. "I can't."

"Can't love me?" he asked. "Or can't say it?" He held his breath, waiting.

Marta pressed her lips together. "Can't lie."

"Good. I find truthful women very sexy." He brushed his lips against hers. "Now tell me."

She knew what he wanted to hear. What *she* had been waiting all her life to hear. To know. "I love you."

He kissed her again, quickly and with feeling. He loved that her eyes looked just the slightest bit dazed. "There, that wasn't so hard, was it?"

She had promised herself never to say those words again, because it hurt so much to have them flung back, disregarded. "Harder than you'll ever know."

He understood. He had a lot of work ahead of him. But nothing he wasn't equal to, or wouldn't enjoy. He was going to spend his life showing her that she had placed her love in the right hands.

"That's because of the past, darlin'. Your past. But this is going to be our future. I swear to you that I'll never do anything to hurt you or make you regret loving me." He smiled into her eyes. "I'm the man you were meant to give your heart to."

She surrendered to the feeling. And to him. Marta

threaded her arms around his neck. "What took you so long?"

He grinned. "We can figure that out on the way back. C'mon, I'm paying Jeb by the half hour. If we don't get back soon, he's going to own the Salty." And then, just as he took her hand to leave the terminal, he stopped abruptly and pulled her back into his arms to kiss her one more time.

She braced her hands against his chest, holding him back. "I thought you were afraid of losing the Salty?"

"Hell, I figure it'll be worth it," he said just before his lips met hers.

* * * * *

Be sure to watch for Luc's romance, coming soon to Silhouette Special Edition.

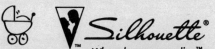

Looking For More Romance?

Visit Romance.net

Look us up on-line at: http://www.romance.net

Check in daily for these and other exciting features:

Hot off the press

View all current titles, and purchase them on-line.

What do the stars have in store for you?

Horoscope

Hot deals

Exclusive offers available only at Romance.net

Plus, don't miss our interactive quizzes, contests and bonus gifts.

PWEB

**Start celebrating Silhouette's 20th anniversary
with these 4 special titles by
New York Times bestselling authors**

*Fire and Rain**
by Elizabeth Lowell

King of the Castle
by Heather Graham Pozzessere

*State Secrets**
by Linda Lael Miller

*Paint Me Rainbows**
by Fern Michaels

On sale in December 1999

Plus, a special free book offer inside each title!

Available at your favorite retail outlet
**Also available on audio from Brilliance.*

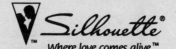

Silhouette®
Where love comes alive™

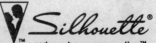